THE
LAYOUT

a storybook

Herbie Johnson

Amazon Book Publication

Copyright © 2024 Herbie Johnson

All rights reserved

The characters and events portrayed in this book are fictitious. Any similarity to real persons, living or dead, is coincidental and not intended by the author.

No part of this book may be reproduced, or stored in a retrieval system, or transmitted in any form or by any means, electronic, mechanical, photocopying, recording, or otherwise, without express written permission of the publisher.

Cover design by the author

Library of Congress Control Number: 2018675309

Printed in the United States of America

For Meredith & Judy

Acknowledgments

The author is indebted to the following literary antecedents, without which The Layout would not have been completed: Chris Baty: No plot? No problem, D J Salinger's Glass family stories, Mary Norton: The Borrowers, T H White: Mistress Masham's Repose, Vladimir Nabokov: Speak, Memory, David Mitchell: Cloud Atlas, Laurence Sterne: The Life & Opinions of Tristram Shandy, Gentleman, Lydia Davis: Collected Stories, Nicholson Baker: The Mezzanine, Catherine Edmunds: Bacchus Wynd, Alain de Botton: How Proust can change your life.

Table of Contents

Dramatis Personae i

I

Harold: I must be dreaming everything into existence 3

Ludwig: Shrapnel-diving 4

Susan Marshwood 5

Olivia: At the supermarket 6

Ben at a bay in Wales 8

Snow White 10

The Burnstone triangle 12

The Selwyn Fussel shop 13

Olivia to Max 15

Ben on the coach 16

Uncle Felix's house 18

MM&V, Sunday morning 19

Harold's unfresh reminiscences 20

Today, Olivia is this way 22

Harold: Bingley Hall 23

A note from Harold 24

The brass Napoleon 26

How to arrange cows 27

II

Mr Fairest's shop 30

Harold: The *Forêt de Broceliande* 31

The old offices 35

You must respect the sea... 36

Lorry 37

At the party 38

The Bad Gödesborg station platform 42

Marginal/peripheral.. 43

Ben in the kitchen 44

Layers of narrative 48

The Burnstone Triangle 49

Margot... 50

III

Model railway people 52

Half-awake again 53

They say, don't they, that to understand everything is to forgive everything?.. 54

Ludwig and his Maman 56

In the cabbage garden 57

Harold: Becoming a municipal Librarian 59

A mysterious stranger 61

Names and stars 62

Olivia Vogel.. 64

Ben on all the toy guns in the house 65

Tinnitus 70

Early days – evolving landscape forms: long-nosed mountain 71

Some dolls are more rigid 72

Nigel Harrison 74

Coin soldiers 75

Prudence and George 76

IV

Olivia's Workroom 79

At the Palace 80

The Three Towns 81

The Original Princess Schneegwyn From 'Way Back 83

The Owl Tea Cosy And The Dolls 85

Well-meaning friends... 86

Platform.. 87

He (who?) idolised his Maman qua the Bugatti Queen 88

A false start 89

The Princess thing.. 90

Ben on the real guns... 91

Fixing the period 94

Two dolls 95

Life on the Layout.. 96

Designing soldiers 98

Scale 101

V

Schnee at the mirror 103

When Downey met Olivia 105

Henrietta tells the tale 107

Tikkun olam 109

French landscape models 110

The road system 111

Here, in a calmer corner of Otto's mind… 112

Rex: Bugatti 113

Europe from the air 114

One-take Rosario, the happy man 115

Ben's Dad on pistols 116

This journal belongs to Margot 117

Downey can't cope 118

1959 119

VI

Ludwig talking to birds 122

Notes on optimum packing 123

Secret nuclear research facility 124

Oh, Jane Burn 125

A wise woman 126

At a boot sale 127

Landscape with Figures 128

Eric's search for order in the universe 129

Therapy 130

Martin 131

Four millimetres to the foot 133

Ben's questions 134

Eric at Sheerness 136

The scruffy area by the brook by the scruffy sheds 137

Harold en route to Venice 138

Martin lost in the Triangle 139

VII

The fortress town of Pignerol in Piedmont 141

From "Optimal Packing and Depletion" (A. R. Davis) 142

The fort in question 143

Eric going to the Kinema 147

The narrator 148

Ludwig's memorandum 150

It's almost 151

Max again 152

Aka cosmic ordering 154

Sparrows 155

Ben at Uncle Felix's 156

Otto's broomstick submarine 164

VIII

There is always a moment of choice 166

Harold at Tesco 167

Let's try to understand Max 169

The Innovative Cheese Products Company 171

Sir Nigel Gresley 172

Ben and the pond 173

Hen's Halloween party 175

Love, as they say, had found him late 178

Harold's intention 179

Renaissance Studies 180

Behind the Colosseum: how Olivia becomes the girl in the photomural in the Costa Coffee shop 181

Felix in wonderland 183

Margot's vocabulary 184

Clocks 186

Notes to self 187

IX

An extraordinary century 189

Is Martin a spy? 190

"Meet me at the Bar Napoleon, and bring the money" 191

Blue Bugatti 192

Amber 193

Jean: A gene for youthfulness? 194

Harold saying the unsaid 195

Eerst Graad 196

Zoë 198

Downey's jokes 200

Prologue 201

The big donkey 203

Harold: The Alabaster incident 204

The two cousins on the platform 206

Harold's book 207

The boys came here on their bikes 210

Whatonages 212

X

Olivia on the bus 215

Mrs Downey's inside 217

England from the air 218

A couple of things may be going on here: 219

Ben on myopia 220

Zozo's Dad 222

Class war comes to the Layout 223

Olivia on art as autobiography 224

Schneegwyn at the hotel 225

The detonation of the bullet 227

Paint and smoke 229

There are times 230

The ducks seem ill at ease 231

Eric's head 232

Harold: Like a séance 233

XI

Max on divinity 235

Harold: Don't forget Fairest's shop 237

Andy on Olivia 238

Poor old General Otto 239

Rex to Max 240

Mother Sparrow and the cat 242

Ben's trouser button 244

Burning decks 245

Ben (as George junior) or indeed Harold 246

Eric's self-justifications 248

Harold: The colours of war 249

I, Olivia 251

Ben: Courtly love 252

Eric on the dolls 253

Planning a party 254

The dimming of the gods 257

XII

Feet of clay 259

ZZZRRT 260

OCD 261

Ben looking in the hotel mirror 262

Dr Downey's animal inventory 263

Harold on religion and rubbish 264

Floaters 266

In the course of one night 267

Olivia and Rex 268

By the pond 269

Understanding Eric 271

Baptised Ludwig 272

Olivia examining Martin 273

Camellia sinensis 274

Counselling 276

Travel light 277

A bedtime story 278

XIII

Chinaman's sleeves 281

A one-sided conversation 282

Olivia up in the air 283

Otto at Bad Gödesborg Station 284

Rex 285

Postscript 286

Susan 288

A dream of winning a million pounds 289

Mistress > shrink 291

Optimum packing 292

A schwa person 293

Something not quite right here 294

He goes through life like Epaminondas in the children's book .. 295

About a toy 296

From Downey's secret journal 298

Ages 300

XIV

Harold is not Max 302

Leaving it for Julia 303

Max: Do I believe in myself? I really do. Am I God? 304

Eggshell-eating Otto 305

Rex, singing in the shower 306

Schnee: Hotels 307

Martin and the talking bee 308

Artists and mirrors 309

The German Submariner's Tale 310

Will the Layout ever be finished? 311

Max's divinity 312

The House of Mothers 313

The Bay Café-Bar 314

For Olivia, it was the dandelions that did it 316

Max drinks 317

On the Yellow River 319

Extraneous matter 320

About The Author 322

THE LAYOUT

a storybook

Dramatis Personae

LOUIS SWANNING, a spoiled & indulged scion of a middle European royal dynasty, is obsessed with playing soldiers with his toy armies but also with his real-life armies.

MARTIN is a railway employee made redundant & spending his time brooding among the cabbages in his cottage garden vegetable plot or wandering about the lanes of the Triangle. He is married to a young mother, JEAN.

SCHNEEGWYN is Jean Rattler's grandmother. In a previous life, she was a middle European princess, heiress to the Bernstein name and fortune, a reincarnation of her namesake who founded the amber mining business.

BEN is a myopic boy, son of Pru & George Harper. His obsessions concern guns and miniature worlds.

DR ERIC DOWNEY, the history teacher, is a bit of a Malvolio figure.

MAX MUNDY is the senior partner in an architectural firm, the father of REX, who is OLIVIA's lover. MAX is God.

OLIVIA VOGEL, the architectural model maker, is also the Holy Spirit to MAX's God. Escaping from an unsuccessful marriage to ANDY, She has a son for whom she began building the layout, but now continues it for her own pleasure & sanity.

FELIX PLUMTREE is BEN's great uncle.

MARGOT GOODE is a troubled girl, the younger cousin of HENRIETTA & ZOE. HENRIETTA SALT is the pretty one.

ZOE PEARCE is the one who will grow up to be a psychotherapist.

GENERAL OTTO VON EISENSCHLUSSEL is a General.

HAROLD THING is writing the book. Only Harold is capable of travelling through time and space.

I

Harold: I must be dreaming everything into existence

Here comes that old scary imminent breakdown feeling again - that because what's happening outside in the world; in my life: the beauty of women, the colour of goldfinches, the taste of Marmite; the existence of black treacle - is so close to what I would hope and fear would be happening, I must be somehow causing it to happen by my thoughts; so if I stop concentrating for even a moment everything's going to collapse into I suppose chaos & the end of the world. And the effort of inventing the future minute by minute as it unfolds is absolutely exhausting & makes me sweat.

Ludwig: Shrapnel-diving

Whenever my Maman's lame older brother, my Onkel Otto, came to visit, he would sit me on his knee and invite me to search through the various little pockets in his tight-fitting General's uniform tunic to find the various coins he called "shrapnel" that he had secreted about his heavily-built person: large brown kopek pieces the size of pennies and the rarer tiny silver groats that would need to be fished out with some difficulty by my small fingers from the fluff and gritty sand that collected in the pocket corners stretched over his hips and thighs.

    Over several years of tea-time visits, I accumulated hundreds of these coins, which I would lay out for inspection in geometric patterns on the dining table like regiments of foot soldiers and their officers. To my five year old imagination, the kopeks were the tightly massed muddy infantry, the silver groats their more mobile commanders free to move about in place on their sometimes skittish white horses at the head of their columns. To me, these were the armies I would one day have at my disposal.

Susan Marshwood

Here's a joyful-looking lady on her bike, shoulder-length blonde-grey hair flying in the breeze, Day-Glo vest flapping. Let's follow her and see where she goes and what she does. I think her name might be Susan Marshwood – as it said on that signpost we passed a couple of miles back, before we stopped to see what the Village Book Fair would be like (a bit of a disappointment – strictly for serious collectors, so no Salinger stories or Patrick White for me, no Barbara Taylor Bradford for you). There she goes, look, freewheeling down the sloping lane, over the odd ramp in the road by the awkward turn where the bridge is, towards that cottage. I bet her daughter lives there with a baby girl – no sign of a son-in-law. She wants to see if there's anything they need from the supermarket or the village shops, then she'll have an excuse to drop in again on her way home, have a coffee, and spend a bit of time playing with the new grand-daughter she never thought she would have. We may meet the daughter again in the café-bar when we get to Lyme Regis. I think she looks like a Jean, or maybe a Mary. Plain-ish, quiet – determined, though. She'll be in there out of the wind, taking her time over feeding the baby. And – oh, I see. The young man with the two dogs, hanging about outside on the prom, is the missing partner. Oh, that's better.

Olivia: At the supermarket

I once met Schneegwyn (known to her friends as Schnee) at the checkouts as she was leaving her till the end of her shift at Morrison's. Still officially listed in The Nobility of Europe as The Princess Schneegwyn Esterhazy-Swanning von Lozin und Bernstein (and people she deals with are wise not to forget it), she is not too proud to use her staff discount card when picking up a few things for dinner. Despite the thick-lensed spectacles she now has to wear to work, she is still recognisably a great if faded beauty and very partial to a nice bit of Haydn.

I am Olivia. I like to dress smartly – oh yes, I suppose it's to please the boss to some extent, but it is mainly for my own satisfaction, and I believe that I work more efficiently if I look and feel efficient and smart. The way I look on the outside has a big effect on the way I feel inside. Makes sense to me. And also, naturally, if the guys find me attractive, they are more likely to take notice of me (though if I overdo it and surprise them, they may be distracted by their own feelings and unable to concentrate on what I'm saying. Men are such boys, and so simple).

But you should see me on my day off. Day off? – what am I thinking! I don't have days off! Firstly, I love my job. Andy used to say I was married to that ber-loody office telephone. And secondly, well, yes, Max is a bit of a slave-driver (in the nicest possible way. It's always in the nicest possible way with Max. In some ways, I wonder if I am in love with the Old Man. He is such a sweetie. But so old-fashioned in some ways. I mean – Homburg hat! Astrakhan collar! What's that all about?

Anyway, I like to think I run a tight ship in the office. I need to know where to find everything – can't be doing with wasting time looking for a file I need. It has to be clearly labelled and know where to file itself. Where it belongs. Like me. And, naturally, in an organisation like MM&V, we need to have order in the warehouse too. Oh, I know Max says, in the end it takes care of itself, but what sort of attitude is that for a boss to take?

I was quite suspicious – why was the boss's son trying to be nice to me? The last time we spent any time alone together was before I had split up with Andy, and when I made it clear to him that I thought he was a thoroughly nice bloke and was happy that we sometimes got to work together and that was fine, but no way was I going to give him any encouragement to try and take things further, he seemed to have kind of accepted that but still sort of closed off that part of his mind. You can see it happen with men, when you do that – you get almost an audible click as that circuit in their brain switches off, if you're lucky – and then you can get on with having a perfectly good working relationship and a new mate you can turn to and talk to when you have to get stuff off your chest, even stuff about other men.

Ben at a bay in Wales

On day one of the holidays, early, a boy is playing on an empty beach. The tide is way out. Deeply firm, deeply damp, the sand the sea seems to leave clean each morning stretches flat and level at the feet of the rock cliffs, unvisited day after day after day except today by this quiet little boy. The Atlantic Ocean, that tickled it clean overnight, and will do so over and over again for aeons, has left a stick in the shape of a Y for the boy to find. One arm of the Y is longer and straight, and soon enough, the boy has poked it into the sand like a pair of compasses or dividers and turned it to scribe himself a perfect circle in the middle of the wide expanse of beach. Then he draws two circles just touching - like snooker balls - adds a third, and contemplates the nature of the triangle: three towns on a map, each with its own circle of influence.

He adds a fourth circle touching two of the three and thinks about the nature of four-sidedness, squareness. Adds a fifth and a sixth and discovers the honeycomb, the hexagon - and soon enough, he finds he is able to draw a perfect nineteen-sixties daisy flower of seven touching circles.

This little quiet bay is just too far from the chalets in one direction, the caravans in the other direction and too inaccessible, looking too uninteresting from the sea to tempt the occasional passing swimmers and canoers and kayakers to come ashore.

What darkness was the boy on the beach getting away from, into his clean salt and sand world of perfect circles and perfect flatness - washed away and new every morning? His tidy abstract patterns? What happens if he adds another touching circle? Spoiled. Start afresh. Add, though - for the beach is wide and empty - another entire ring of circles skirting a new flower, and what happens? Soon enough, so long as each new circle touches two already there, sets of straight lines of circles begin to stretch away in two (or is it three?) directions across the beach, reaching towards what? This way, the dark cliffs; that way, the open sea. Beyond that? Infinity? A puzzle. The boy contemplates his pattern for a while and scoots off home to his uncle Felix's little wooden house for a late breakfast but no telling off.

One day, he may find a way to make himself a star.

Snow White

The family myth was that either Schnee herself or one of her ancestors – someone somewhere way back in the mists of time. I dunno, fifteenth or sixteenth century, I suppose, thinking about it, if not earlier – had been the precious princess daughter of the King or Baron or Duke or whatever of a little kingdom hidden away among the wildwood of central Europe. Austria or Hungary or somewhere, in the days before the Hapsburgs, was it, had unified it all into an empire. So – the fairy tale times, really, like in the pantomimes, and a time of myths. There had been for centuries rumours of prodigal creatures glimpsed living in the forest - Schneegwynn's amber-mining dwarfs, of course, but also a great donkey christened at various times Titan, Goliath, Hercules or Meaulnes.

Anyway…the princess's father was hard up and so, naturally enough, wanted to find a favourable marriage for his daughter. Either that or there was a terrible epidemic – plague or something, even just rats, maybe. And anyway, along comes Ludwig, or Louis if you prefer…and it was not him the brass statuette was of – the one as kids we all used to think was just a bad likeness of Napoleon. Any road up, to cut a long story short, Ludwig carried granny's granny off to his own little kingdom in the depths of the forests, where they lived happily ever after. Only it wasn't ever after.

For a start, they were cousins, and they probably shouldn't really have been allowed to get married, and then when they did have a child, it had something wrong with it…and so did the next child…and another…and eventually they were so miserable that Ludwig couldn't bear it and he left her to deal with it all herself. Which was not much fun, but she was made of sterner stuff, or the iron entered her soul or something…anyway, it made her a formidable woman...

And then one day, wandering about in the rocky woods in her solitary misery, she picked up a piece of amber in the forest. I don't know, maybe she had a little dog with her, and he brought it up out of a rabbit hole – or she may have had a big deerhound, something rough-coated and impressive but gentle that might have helped look after the poor ugly children, and the dog showed the children the rabbit hole and they went down it and found more pieces of amber…and the rest is history. They showed the hole to Granny Schnee, and they all put their heads together, eventually they set up the mines, and it became the biggest amber-digging operation in the world. Something like that. Probably.

The Burnstone triangle

This is a landscape you could walk into (never mind that the geology is offcut polystyrene) if you were twenty millimetres tall. Three place names on the map enclose the stretch of countryside where trains no longer run, though still waited for by the somehow Welsh twins on the platform and looked out for by the guy in the vegetable patch beyond the fence waving his red-spotted kerchief while his tiny wife pegs out her tiny washing.

The Selwyn Fussel shop

Inspiration came to Olivia in the wind on a windy night, and when she went out the next morning to explore her new surroundings, everything in her life looked different and had changed in a million small ways and many large ways. It was as if in some dream world, she had chosen voluntarily to hang by her foot from the tree Yggdrasil and had gained a new way of looking at the world, a new currency (and indeed, the old coins had fallen from her pocket and were lost, but her kind new employer had arranged an advance for her, so confident was he that she was the woman for the job, and in order to make her feel valued and comfortable here).

She imagined a universe in which people liked and understood what she was doing – where she was the capable and practical right hand of a benevolent God. Then God took early retirement. She nurses a suspicion that she is not a very nice person – has she not taken advantage of Max's affection and now of Rex's likewise?

Here was a Selwyn Fussel model shop – so everything was going to turn out all right.

She had that feeling of sand under her nails that she remembered from the dream last night when she (oh, yes...it started to come back to her now) had been busily making the models.

She needed to drive a car (preferably a nice red sports car, but not a Bugatti) and to get a map of the town. When she gets back to the big house, she will write to her son and tell him – and us – what is going on: how Andy, her husband, is history and how she is once more enjoying working on the layout they used to enjoy building together when he - and she, of course - was younger).

Olivia to Max

ROME

Dear Max,

This may come as a surprise. I got a spur-of-the-moment invitation to join Rex here. Sorry if this doesn't fit in with any plans you might have had for me this weekend. Please let me know if there are any problems in this part of the world that I could be looking at while I'm here.

He seems to think you want him to see about opening a branch here in Italy.

I know you said we mustn't let on to anyone who we really are, but are you absolutely certain that's the best way?

Ben on the coach

Here comes the Welcome to Hampshire sign, and the bus rattles round a bend down a lane marked Paradise. A village whose main claim to fame – apart from its famous view of the green hillside and distant lake – is that its little High Street is home to the offices of Mundy, Mundy and Vogel. Max, Rex and Olivia work here. People never actually ask Olivia, "So how does it work – do you just ring him and say, I need a cheque for fifteen million pounds, and he just signs it?" – which might be just as well since they might not believe the simplicity of the answer. There is a car park to the rear of the building, accessed through the carriage archway of the former coaching inn – the Lamb and Flag, with room for up to three clients to park their cars, but no one has ever been seen driving in or out of it except desperate tourists who have lost their way. Inter-office memos of a kind flit between the offices occupied by Olivia, Max and Rex, and yet the firm's stationery bill is negligible. If this is too much of a mystery – don't worry about it. All will become as clear as it needs to be, in due course. In the meantime, we have a small boy in need of some self-confidence.

Ben had got himself safely onto the right coach when the bus dropped him off at Digbeth, and had done the same again when the first coach pulled into the coach station at Cheltenham after an uneventful trip that dutifully provided the statutory first views of fields with horses and black-and-white cows a mile or so south of

Redditch. Now, he was getting tired with the excitement of being allowed to travel on his own and the strain of paying attention when the coach was moving to ensure he didn't miss a single moment of the passing scenery. He rested his forehead against the window and gazed out dreamily at the woodland the coach was passing through, trying to remain alert in case he should catch sight of a green-clad outlaw flitting between the trees or maybe a small hand-picked squad of commandos deployed in a rocky ravine.

The young man (is he eight? No – he has been allowed by his mother, in discussion with his uncle, to travel alone from Birmingham to Dorset. He is at least ten, but in fact, I don't need to specify: his thoughts and preoccupations will show [not tell] the reader his age). And, speaking of William Tell, he also might appear among the trees. At length, the green country bus into which he has now been decanted makes its rattling way through village after village (half the time feeling to the young man as if it must be going in completely the wrong direction) and comes to Uncle Felix's house.

Uncle Felix's house

At Felix's house, there was gas lighting - Ben had been given instruction, on his first visit, to be very careful when lighting the gas jets not to touch the gas mantles – those little fragile white things like miniature white woolly hats that somehow contained the flame so it glowed orange instead of burning blue, and that stopped the whole of the gas in the pipes from igniting and sending the entire place up in flames – when putting a match to them.

And then there was the year he arrived at Uncle Felix's for the summer holidays, to be greeted by a face like thunder again – but more in sadness than in anger – and the axe and saw to deal with the pine tree he had killed by ring-barking it the previous summer.

There was a faded and, I think, very imperfectly printed Chinese block-print bedspread at Uncle Felix's house. At home, Ben had an eiderdown; I think it was printed with "modern" abstract multi-coloured Kandinskyesque and amoeba-like brightly-coloured shapes in which he used to see all kinds of pictures when he was not simply imagining it as hills and valleys as it was draped over the geological rocks of his knees.

MM&V, Sunday morning

The architects are having cottage cheese bagels and coffee at a table on the cobblestones outside the café in the town square. Rex has parked his sky-blue Bugatti under the plane tree – he can never manage to manoeuvre it into the official MM&V parking space in the courtyard of their offices. It's possible that Mary Mundy, Max's "Armenian" wife, has joined them.

Talk turns to a discussion between God the Father, God the Son and God the Holy Ghost of the state of the world they create, created and continuously create: how foolish, fearful but wonderful people have turned out to be, etc. And how the people are also continuously creating the world they see and how that seems a great mystery.

The architects - Max, Rex and Olivia – used to get together every Friday afternoon for a post-mortem on the week's business. This tradition began in the early days when, as Mundy, Mundy and Vogel, the firm had its offices round the courtyard - the days before the Stockroom became, for a while, The Universal Emporium, before morphing into the much more relaxed and fantastic/incredible source of material that enabled the Layout to become what it did.

Harold's unfresh reminiscences

While I was still at school, my sisters were both working in public libraries and would bring home back issues of a magazine entitled Books and Bookmen. Not unlike the latter-day Poetry Book Society Review, Books and Bookmen always featured on its front cover a photograph (in black and white – which I fancy added to the specialness of the image (or maybe not, in those days. This would have been some time in the late nineteen fifties when I suppose colour photos on magazine covers were quite a rarity). Whatever – in retrospect, and at the time, the point is, these were highly glamorous images. There would be – and I'm working hard here – J.B. Priestley with a pipe in his mouth, Aldous Huxley perhaps, Doris Lessing. It was, I think in the days before Margaret Drabble, Margaret Attwood or A.S. Byatt. Iris Murdoch could have been there, and maybe Lawrence Durrell. You get the picture. It's not crucial (though it may be significant) that I forget who I saw month after month – or was it week after week? Surely not. The point is that this was Litporn but it was at the same time Glamour. This was also a kind of understated and cultured fame, endorsed by the approval of my family, that I might aspire to. Thus, was conceived in my early teenage brain the notion that I would like to become a Novelist.

It was the time when I was being put under pressure to decide on a career path. Obviously, in view of the family imperative to not be unoriginal, I was not at that stage prepared to take to librarianship like my sisters. Teaching (which most of my peers – having no imagination as far as I could see - seemed to think was the obvious route to prosperity and fulfilment) was also out, not least because I had no respect whatsoever for the general run of teachers I had encountered. Work in a bookshop, obviously, beckoned.

Today, Olivia is this way

Yesterday she was...Tomorrow she will be...They are all different, but she is all of them, and they are all Olivia. "I am human. I contain multitudes"

"My name is Legion."

Turning inward more and more since she and Andy split up, and now Andrew has finished Uni and got his own place, she spends her days trying to breathe life into her layout.

The big house had been shut up for so long that the mirrors in the amber-lined Long Gallery had given up reflecting, but soon, they would begin again to enjoy showing Olivia herself dashing past them between antique glass cases containing ranks of model soldiers and the lives of Hannibal, Bellerophon and Epaminondas.

Harold: Bingley Hall

As a boy, I wanted a proper electric Hornby Dublo '00' gauge railway layout from the time I first saw one in action at, probably, Bingley Hall, where we used to go with half the population of the city a couple of times a year for the Ideal Homes Exhibition. There would always be a man in shirtsleeves demonstrating the orange juice extractor – a sharp-edged tube of either white metal or, more recently, transparent amber-coloured plastic that he screwed into the side of an orange which he proceeded to squeeze and massage over a clear jug, that filled up with always a surprising volume of juice that we bystanders were invited to taste.

A note from Harold

I can't shake the Schnee name (though I did kind of vow in my writer's manifesto not to use weird sci-fi type names or Russian-type names because they irritate and confuse me so much and would presumably also confuse my readers. Schnee (really Schneegwyn, known as Schnee - pronounced Shnay by anyone in the know) has to be the exception. She's meant to be a matriarch along the lines of Maggie Smith in Downton Abbey but very much more Central European from way back and of an uncertain generation, consequently easily and often conflated and/or confused in the minds of her descendants when re-telling her exploits to each other and their children, with her great great grandmother (of the same name). Also of course, she is on one level Snow White. She is clearly the symmetrical-faced pretty young girl with a baby I noticed in Hodges restaurant, though the ages may not fit: she could at a pinch have been in her twenties – I can never, well hardly ever, guess women's ages. Heck, quite often I can't even be certain whether a woman I see in two different photos – or, yes, come to that, in two different outfits – are one and the same or not. It's like that thing ole Shakespeare says in Antony and Cleopatra about her "something something infinite variety". There was a young man and a child at the table with her – initially, I assumed she and the child were sisters, but she could have been the young mother.

People who are not in the know or part of the charmed circle of the family sometimes assume, when they hear Schnee addressed as what sounds like shnay, that her name is Sinead. Some of the family take delight in fostering confusion of this sort among those they feel to be outsiders.

The brass Napoleon

In a tiny backstreet brass foundry in the Jewellery Quarter of Birmingham late in the nineteenth century, a workman at the end of his shift indulged a bright-eyed young boy. Together, they weighed out pink copper shavings and the soft, dull scraps of tin, made a plaster mould from the hand-high figurine the boy's old uncle had left him, and carefully poured in the bright liquid metal from the crucible. Not quite enough, so the casting would need a foot fashioned from wax if it was ever to stand upright. But it would be treasured for years despite its lame imperfection – like the Brave Tin Soldier in the fairy tale book.

How to arrange cows

In a way that will conceal the fact that they are largely identical.

Olivia was feeling excited. She had finally put the black and white cows - all of them - in the top field that sloped up to the edge of the trees, and they were looking good. A few were clustered by the gate as if hoping for some further human attention, but most had headed off in a loose group to explore their new surroundings. She decided to get a few more from the same supplier.

The landscape she is actually modelling is metaphysical. Like the creation of a dolls' house, the purpose is not to finish or complete it…it is a place for contemplation. Which reminds me - Olivia keeps parked in a barn behind one of the sheds by the stream at Fussel Darcy, an old charabanc, in case she wants to travel back to the, I suppose, the late twenties/early thirties.

Olivia is incredibly well-read. She goes through life like the proverbial White Tornado. She just returned from the USA where she read her poems and gave a series of writing workshops. She has a husband somewhere in Plymouth but hardly ever mentions him or sees him, as far as we can tell.

She was left the big house by an ancient uncle. Originally a stately country home, it has been through many incarnations, and was for many years the Bullfinch Retreat, a refuge for perplexed gentlefolk founded there in the eighteenth century or even earlier.

Last I heard, the grounds were being used for paintball weekends. Olivia lets out part of the house to some team-building outfit but lives in the top two or three floors.

She is well aware that what you expect to happen, happens.

II

Mr Fairest's shop

Little old Mr Fairest didn't wear a cow gown, though they were for sale in the shop next to his toy shop. Cow gown is what the local country people called the long tan overall coat worn by the cowmen who drove the cows into the milking parlour twice a day.

The two images – of the cow gowns for sale in the window of the Gentlemen's Outfitters and of Mr Fairest in his shop selling me obsolete Minic Motorways vehicles and accessories – sit side by side in my memory.

His stock was old stock even then, and I never saw anyone else in his shop. I think he was deaf, and he used to let me have things for good prices as if he didn't expect to make any profit but simply wanted to get rid of the leftover things.

Harold: The *Forêt de Broceliande*

When we went to the Loire, incognito, and again a couple of years later in Brittany in search of the Forêt de Broceliande, there were displays in some of the chateaux about life in the Middle Ages. We also came across a more or less derelict castle being carefully rebuilt by archaeologists using only the building techniques that would have been available in the Middle Ages. I have photos I took. And I recently, in my bookshelves, came across my notebook from that period. It's a bit scribbled, having been written on the bus, I expect. You can't quite make out all the words, but it seems to say…

What did the barons do?

Barons maintained one or more castles as military strong points. They controlled lands and forests and collected taxes to support their activities. They were subject to the King's laws as they...

Why is baron court called baron court?

Originally, in the olden days, a king could rule with barons, who ruled the more day-to-day problems of their times. They could go to war, negotiate peace, or execute someone in a barons court.

What are Barons?

Baron. A Baron is a rank of nobility, originally a tenant holding land directly from the monarch.

In the Middle Ages, women died young. Births were often lethal.

Men soon remarried. It was frequent for a princess to live with a reconstituted family.

Many fairy tales describe cruel stepmothers who try to get rid of the children from their husband's first union. History also mentions assassin stepmothers, but most of them gave princesses the love of a real mother.

In all the stages of a princess's life, the family would decide her fate. A young noble girl would marry around the age of twelve. This was too serious a business to give room to feelings.

In the Middle Ages, princesses of royal blood of each generation formed a small circle of about thirty women. They would not all become queens, but they all knew one another because they belonged to the same family. They were all the same because their fate was the same.

A birth was always a cause for celebration regardless of whether the child was a boy or a girl, But a boy was better accepted. A boy would inherit the family's property. A boy would become King. In France, a girl had no access to the throne and could not transmit the throne to her son.

The princess would soon be baptised, and a prestigious godfather or godmother would be chosen for her.

As soon as she was born, a princess lived in a luxurious environment. Her ceremonial cradle was garnished with fur. When she was still very young, she was left in the custody of a nanny and a lullaby singer. The men of her family attended to her to protect her until marriage.

The housekeeper was a noble lady who had been selected for her good temperament and morality. Her parents were often away, minding political and military business.

From the 12th century, treatises of education were published on a regular basis. They all agreed on three principles: princesses had to be subordinate to men; they embodied the family's honour and had to be models to other women.

Women are Eve's daughters. Sinful beings who lead men astray.

A princess had to be under the supervision and obey the men of her family, who, according to their own interests, chose her husband, who would then dominate her too.

Such submission to men implied the observance of a code of conduct.

The princess received education as to her body, which distinguished her from other women. She would always stand straight and immobile. Her eyes would always look half closed.

She would walk with little short steps without looking around herself. She would not speak publicly because a woman's word was just considered as lies and gossip.

She cried in silence and never laughed.

A princess received a very comprehensive education to become a learned woman. In the Middle Ages, young girls were better educated than boys who, from the age of 7, trained to become knights.

Her chaplain and the ladies in her surroundings gave her a religious and moral education. At the age of six. she would learn how to read and write, how to count and calculate.

She minded her own brothers and sisters to learn how to become a mother. She would weave and embroider with other women to avoid idleness, the source of evil.

Before the age of ten, she would leave her relatives to join either a convent or the King's Court or her in-laws when she was already engaged.

The little princess also had to shine at the King's Court.

She had to play music, dance and read poetry.

She also had to know how to catch hawks and be a good rider.

For a noble family, the marriage of a daughter was the opportunity to conclude new alliances. By marrying his daughter, the king could reward a faithful great vassal, enlarge his kingdom or bail out his coffers. Daughters were like pawns manipulated according to their father's needs. Marriages were also a way of sealing peace treaties.

As heir of the former kings of Brittany, Francois II did not consider himself a vassal to the King of France. If he wanted to remain independent, his daughter was his only asset.

A princess did not choose her own husband. Her family or the king decided for her when she was a little girl. There was no place for love. If the princess was in love with someone else, they had to escape to make a secret marriage.

Once they got married, the couple learned to know each other. The princess did not see her husband often because he was often travelling for his affairs. The princess wished to expect a baby quickly to give a son to the kingdom, who became king later.

When the king died, and his son was too young, the queen governed the kingdom in his place. She became regent. When her son was old enough to govern, she had to give up the power.

<<Ta vie de princesse, en fait c'est quoi?>> se dit-elle en elle-même.

<<Supporter cette lourde couronne que l'on va m'obliger de porter ou si je ne fais pas d'enfant mâle, je serai déchue, d'un revers de main.

Alors, il ne me reste plus que le choix de subir, victime d'être la fille d'un roi ou l'épouse d'un prince...>>

The old offices

A tall clean modernistic building of many, many stories, built of what looked like white shining stone. And next to it, a nondescript, ramshackle edifice with a brass plate in need of a good polish:

MUNDY, MUNDY & VOGEL, ARCHITECTS

At seven-thirty on a Monday morning, before anyone had arrived at the offices - not even the postman - a crumpled ball of paper materialized in the wire cage inside the letterbox.

By a quarter to nine – a time that went on sometimes for a couple of hours, being Max's favourite time of day when he felt he was on his own time (a laughable concept if you think about it – all time is his after all), and was doing the firm a favour by attending to work things when he didn't have to, and could therefore do them in his own way and take as long as he wished to in order to take that little extra care – the crumpled message was flattened out on Max's desk blotter. He was reading it through for the second time as he waited for his coffee to cool in the "World's Best Dad" mug that Rex had given him at Christmas.

You must respect the sea

*When I was young
my mother told me the story
of a sailor who falls overboard:
the mermaid always asks him
- "Who is King?"
Unless he answers, 'Alexander
the Great' she lets him drown.*

(Katerina Neocleous)

The German submariner who appears later in this book could be General Otto witnessing sea trials of a new submarine and getting washed overboard. The sea monster could well be a "mermaid" and could ask him the Alexander question once a year (until he gets it right), and he could end up running a pushbike and moped hire shop somewhere on the West African coast.

Lorry

There goes the dark green lorry, down to the quayside, predictable as clockwork. Who's driving, and what is it carrying every day?

At the party

120 School Road was a typical bit of lower middle-class Victorian housing, in the shadow of the red brick spire of the local high gothic revival church.

Henrietta and Zoë were in the back room, setting up a white sheet hung by drawing pins from the doorway leading into the hall. They had a bowl, a flashlight and a wet sponge. While people waited to bob for apples and watched others getting half drowned in the enamel bucket, they would be gigglingly invited to 'follow the moon with their nose' as the flashlight was moved up and down and across behind the sheet. After a couple of minutes, at what seemed the appropriate moment, the victim would be led to follow the 'moon' to the edge of the sheet and be treated to a splash of cold, wet sponge in the face before being offered a towel and the laughing sympathy of previous victims who had stayed to watch their discomfiture.

Schnee was talking to – or possibly at – Margot on the sofa. "Hector was in love with Harriet Smithson you see, had been for years. But eventually, he met Estelle when she was an old lady, and obviously, he was quite an old man too. In his eyes, Harriet became Estelle. Or do I mean Estelle became Harriet for him? Anyway, he loved her." No visible response. Margot's eyes were glazed again.

"Of course, my father loves all the complications," Rex was telling Olivia. "I know, as head of the firm, he feels he ought to be detached and efficient and a bit of a machine, but – take this thing of the finches, for instance. He couldn't get enough of colour-charts and dissertations on the way the eyes work – all that stuff that would have left me cold. A paper-clip counter, that guy. Hasn't got the broader picture at all."

"Not true," she said. "There's more to him than that. He's a very complicated man. God, this is boring. Why is it that we always end up talking about Max? Let's get another drink."

By the time she came back to the settee with their glasses refilled, he had moved on to another topic. "The fourth dimension is time. We all know about that. It goes forward, never back–time flies like an arrow, and all that. When you enter the fifth dimension, you can look at what's going on in the other four from the outside, a bit like Einstein's observer watching the two trains. It's as if you went out of the house by the front door, leaving a party in full swing in the front room. You could hear the party going on, but you wouldn't be part of it. Then, if you walked round and came in through the kitchen door, you would find a totally different scene, where maybe someone might be lying dead on the floor. And it would be a different story and a different time – well, it could be. Earlier or later. Hey, that's a thought – I wonder if it might be possible to split and inhabit two different universes at the same time. Or two different bodies in one universe. Of course, you couldn't be conscious of being both at the same time – you'd probably go mad…"

"Hmm…," said Olivia, "I know there are supposed to be an infinite number of universes, parallel ones to this, each slightly different. Is that what they call alternative reality?"

"Well, in some of them, life is not supposed to have evolved. So there is no one to observe them. But the theory is that if no one observes them, they don't really exist."

"And yet the observer alters what he sees, don't they say?" She twirled a stray tendril of hair. "I suppose if there is no one to see, then it's like Schrödinger's cat, and it's not possible to say what it's like – dead or alive."

"Or not there at all. And in fact, the thing about the real world is that it is so complex we can't describe it. And, anyway, each observer sees the same thing differently – because of their slightly different viewpoint as well as the different life experiences they bring with them, that colour their perception."

"Phew. I need some air. Coming?"

"Rex, Rex," thought Susan, overhearing their conversation through the open door of the next room, "why do you always have to talk to her as if you were a physics textbook?"

Later, in the garden, Olivia was trying yet again to explain double-entry book-keeping to him, and while she talked, her fingers were idly picking the yellow petals one by one from a spike of evening primrose that was growing alongside the bench, putting them alternately onto two piles on the seat beside her...A lot of the time, there was literally an Alp between her and Rex, she thought, and she despaired of knowing what he really thought. Or felt.

Eric was pontificating to Henrietta, who was not listening but was nonetheless beaming at him as if entranced: "Europe at the start of the eighteenth century I described as a continent at war with itself. Not original, of course."

"Such a troubled childhood," she was thinking as she let his words flow over her, and, "From darkness into light." She turned on him those china-blue eyes, the same eyes that will one day be miraculously preserved with a misleading label in some museum or other in a Paris basement.

"The songs of the nightingale, quail and cuckoo."

"You're a big baby. It's time you learned to speak proper English."

"And finally, in my life, I find myself, for whatever reason being treated with kindness by my wife."

"But don't think I can't see through your little schemes."

"If this is going to work, it's gonna hurt."

"This is my hubbie, Mr Bland (I have made him what he is). He does everything for me now."

"She is a true princess, but also a real farmer's daughter. If you lend her anything, don't expect to ever see it again. I gave her my trust – and I did once upon a time lend her my heart."

". . . and it's important that you don't fall in love with me. I would love you to fall in love with me, but I've stopped trying to make it happen. Even though it seems only fair, it would not be a good idea for you to fall in love with me."

"But you don't want to be a railway porter all your life, do you – even if they do give you a jacket and a hat with a braid on it?"

"It's a job, Mother."

All this talk, all these words and thoughts, and a seemingly infinite stream of others were rising in the evening air over the houses. Witches and ghosts and apple-bobbing had been forgotten. Young Ben was tucked up asleep in his absent cousin John's narrow bed, dreaming of following the moon with his nose. The dog was asleep on the tartan blanket across his feet. Tomorrow, Ben was going to be allowed to explore the attic with Auntie Winnie. She had promised.

The Bad Gödesborg station platform

Is a-buzz with people who come from miles around on the strength of a rumour first carried into the region by the carter's boy, who can read, and swiftly propagated by the matrons of the villages and their daughters who remember the handsome young officer, fresh from the military academy, whom they waved off to war all those years before. Can it really be only four years? So much has changed – the railway has come, of course, but also this thing called a Fernsprecher that lets you hear people talking in far distant towns, and electric lights, and motor carriages, and machine guns, and wireless – and the train pulls in and eventually a carriage door opens. A great gasp goes up from the crowd – his whiskers that the girls used to so admire for their virile form and coaly blackness are indeed now snowy white, transformed, so it is whispered, by the horrors he has had to witness in the trenches. And that distinguished limp and the silver top of his cane – and ah! His poor shattered ankle!

Marginal/peripheral

Max set up the conditions that allow Olivia, as his handmaiden and consort/co-regent/agent, to maintain (albeit in her own sometimes offhand or distracted manner) the life of the Layout. And at some point, he bequeathed to her the big old house when she was in need of a place to live.

His main concerns are other, elsewhere, larger and incomprehensible to the Layout's inhabitants. Denizens is an appealing word.

Ben in the kitchen

George junior (Ben to you) remembers the bottom cupboards. Ben used to spend his early years getting under his mother's feet in the kitchen at 356 Clay Lane. She would be busy preparing food or whatever, and he would have the doors of one or other of the floor-level cupboards open, rummaging. The left-hand cupboard, which was the bottom of the kitchen cabinet, contained the big saucepans – lovely noisy things that, with a wooden spoon would keep him happy for hours – not to mention the other assorted bits of seldom-used kitchen equipment (nameless fascinating-shaped blocks of wood, slightly rusted tin or steel containers and weird old-fashioned implements with knobs or handles) that had drifted down there like pieces of scree from a glacier, over the years.

The right-hand cupboard was the shoe cupboard. Not sure on what basis shoes arrived down here. Certainly, most of Ben's Dad's everyday shoes lived there – brown dried-out-looking things with laces, that would be fished for just before going out. "Fished for" because people seemed to just sling their shoes in here higgledy-piggledy, with no idea of tidiness or even, really, keeping them in pairs – much less of segregating one person's footwear from another person's. Because five people lived in this house – Mummy and Daddy, Ben himself, and his two older sisters – Joyce aka Adja (also known, I gather, as Jam Jar, for reasons I'll probably mention later) and Evangeline, usually called Eva but (I learned later, as will you) christened Eva Brick by one of our zombie schoolteachers. All three offspring went, in due course, to the same grammar school in Birmingham.

I mention the shoes because young Ben revealed one aspect of his true nature quite early on in life by adopting the role of polisher to the family – that being, I suppose, a pretty harmless but easily mastered set of skills. Certainly he was most of the time biddable and, given the necessary time, would happily be of service in waxing and buffing a pair of shoes on request before one of the others had to go out. And on the days when Mummy was in a dusting mood, Ben would often get the job of polishing either furniture or brass ornaments or both.

The back door led from the kitchen via two or three (two I think) brick steps into what was known as The Shed. For long stretches of our childhood, this was a tricky place to negotiate, for a few reasons. Our father, whose primary realm The Shed seemed to be, was not only a man of wide and varied interests. He was also undeniably untidy and a hoarder of anything that might come in useful someday, or that was remotely 'interesting'. And, his interests ran to the mechanical, the metal and the frankly unclean. Taking a basket of freshly-laundered, damp washing out, to the clothes-line that ran along the right-hand path in the back garden, through the dark and often oily Shed, past any number of precariously-piled up and projecting pieces of nameless mechanism that Dad had picked up from unimaginable scrap-yards or worse during his work in the Jewellery Quarter and such places, would be a hazardous and, for our mother, exasperating, experience. "Exasperating" was a word with which the infant Ben became familiar early on, as was also "provoke," as in "don't provoke your sister".

The back garden is a whole other realm, which we may be exploring later in this narrative. Suffice it for now, probably, to say that although Ben's Mother was keen to have a "nice" garden, and would at various times enjoy pottering and tending, in particular, her beloved rose bushes, neither of the parents was a committed or systematic gardener, and Dad was only infrequently persuaded to do much work on the plants. Ben's memories of Dad gardening were largely concerned with him struggling to tame various very spiky bushes and to keep intact or restore to intactness the assorted runs of somewhat random kinds of fencing that, over the years, attempted to frustrate various pet rabbits, dogs and tortoises from exploring the wider neighbourhood – all too often accompanied by a litany of "blasted"s and other mutterings. Ben's Dad often found life not only frustrating and exasperating but also 'provoking' in the extreme.

The other door from the kitchen led, of course, via the hall alongside the stairs, to the front door, passing the doors to the "Garden Room," as the rear living room was grandly called, and the front room (normally reserved for use at Christmas or for entertaining the occasional 'posh' visitor – though it later served as a bedsitter for a while and was the setting for occasional games. The hall was, at least in the early years, floored with linoleum of a dull pink – excellent for sliding along in socks.

At home, on the mantelpiece used to stand propped up a brass statuette of Napoleon with one foot missing. I have no idea why our parents should have given house room to such an item.

In the ramshackle/tumbledown shed/garage a small vice, bolted to a solid bench, serves the boy as an anvil when he hammers pins to make tiny cutlass blades, slides on a quarter-inch of red, black or green electric flex insulation to serve as a grip and impales another sideways for a guard and crosspiece. He doesn't know whether the tiny people will come if he makes ready tiny living or hiding places underground with food and weapons, but he knows it's important to believe they will. What kind of food will be suitable? Peas, cheese, sultanas, small dry biscuits (Iced Gems – they will like the little swirls of hard icing, too.)

I'm simply Ben. I can tell you what I did and thought at various ages and what I have been told. But I can't tell you for sure what is going on in other people's heads – though I can imagine or make an educated guess – or what happens in the next room. Only in this one.

Layers of narrative

A collection of journals?

    Ben's recollections;

    Harold on how he is writing his book;

    Max on how the universe is put together;

    Olivia on getting out of a relationship and on building a layout;

    Rex on being in love with a woman and a car;

    Otto on having a smashed ankle;

    Martin or Eric on the dolly cousins;

    Ludwig or his tailor on Ludwig and the war;

    and so on.

The Burnstone Triangle

Has one side or corner on the coast so that there can be deckchairs and a sea view. And, of course, one side also on the edge of the enormous mid-European forests where much happens in the past.

Margot

Once upon a time there was a little girl who lived with her Mummy and Daddy in a nice big house in the middle of a town.

Margot feels okay, though she gets very nervous and uptight because she often misses what is going on and misunderstands people's motives and intentions and is aware she seems different from most people. But she's been over-protected, poor thing, so she can't help it. But some kind of revelation and breakthrough is going to happen somewhere sometime – even she feels that.

I remember, says Margot, the toy butcher's shop, or at least the painted plaster cuts of meat, the little golden-tinged ham with the little loop of wire to hang it from the steel rail in the shop window, or from the beam in the doll's house kitchen; the pies and sides of beef, and sausages like bunches of pink bananas. And ah, now I can see again the catalogues Mother let me have, how I would sit quietly for hours carefully cutting out little pictures of pairs of shoes, and saucepans, bird cages and suitcases. The reason I did it escapes me, though I suppose it was simple enough. What is it Freud said – the id is satisfied by the image of the thing it desires? Something like that, and looked at another way, of course, my mother was simply beginning my training to become a little consumer, a capitalist child.

III

Model railway people

Nigel's Dad had made him a model railway layout up in the attic. Nigel, by the time Ben knew him, seemed pretty bored with actually playing with it – more interested in telling Ben how many model locos he had got and how expensive they had been, but what took Ben's attention was the little figure of an off-duty railway porter tending the rows of tiny French Knots of cabbages in the garden of his lineside railway company cottage. The little man in waistcoat and shirtsleeves was leaning on his tiny rake, trying not to breathe as if waiting for the boys to go back down the ladder, close the trapdoor and let him get on with his double-0 scale life.

Nigel's Dad might have arranged for the attic light to automatically switch off when the trap door closed, but we have no proof that happened.

Half-awake again

Harold is lying half-awake with his eyes closed, wondering about a syndrome where you fall in love with your servants and lose them one by one to other servants or their masters; wondering about Mrs Thing's schwa syllable . . . it represents a noncommittal response and drives Harold crazy - though he can understand how it might have developed: there have been times and situations in his own life when any response to a question has felt dangerous and likely to provoke a violent or unpleasant reaction. His Dad used to say "Yes, Dear," in the interest of a quiet life. He himself tended to ask what felt to him like intelligent questions seeking further information before deciding - which more often than not merely served to annoy his interlocutor and further inflame a volatile moment.

Harold realises he is a creature of habit: he survives in this world through a series of rituals that allow him to function every day without thinking - his mind elsewhere.

Harold is possessed of a terrible hunger to understand things - appropriate when he was Ben, aged four, perhaps, but in an adult of advanced years a recipe for daily frustration, even when he rules enormous fields of knowledge (economics, pure mathematics, sport, theoretical physics - if there is such a thing) to be out of bounds.

They say, don't they, that to understand everything is to forgive everything?

In that spirit - since I need at this distance in time to try to forgive him – let me try to tell you about Eric, or Doctor Downey, as I would have called him at the time. My first impression of him was that his suit was too tight. Memory shows him to me in a yellowish greeny tweed suit, presumably a three-piece and probably the genuine expensive article – the kind of tweed that smells faintly of wee when it gets wet (due to the dye having been fixed in the wool with some kind of urine-based mordant). The yellowish greeny note relates to his presumed love life, the Malvolio thing that in my mind has him besotted with Henrietta in an absolutely hopeless way and trying to impress her by, as it were, wearing yellow tights cross-gartered to the knee in green. Doctor Eric Downey was my grammar school history teacher. His ambition at that time was apparently to persuade a class of maybe thirty assorted young Brummie boys and girls to memorize lists of the names and dates of battles in the Napoleonic and other wars. I dare say he thought he was making history come alive for us in the way it clearly did for him as he strutted up and down at the front of the bored class, acting out the swagger of Bismarck as he rattled his imaginary sabre in its imaginary scabbard. I just thought he was a pompous idiot, though later, after hearing his cinema anecdote, that impression became tinged with pity. And now, thirty years on, I begin to piece together what his hopes and fears and failed ambitions might have been – what might have made him the way he was.

In the movie of this book, Eric would ideally have been played by Philip Seymour Hoffman.

Ludwig and his Maman

His Maman's boudoir is where he learns to wheedle...to wheedle and also to sulk, prettily.

His beloved Maman taught him words such as embonpoint.

He does not know the meaning of everything she says, but he loves to hear her voice: enjoys the sound and misses it when she is not speaking to him (he is entranced by the sound, will sit at her feet and listen happily even when she is speaking to someone else, even in one of the half dozen of her languages he does not yet understand. To him, it is like listening to the music played by a tiny French chamber band - viola, cello, oboe and bassoon, that would perform to a dozen or so of his relations and hangers-on in one of the rooms of the palace a few times a year).

He didn't feel his day could properly begin until she was awake and had spoken to him. Had given him a morning kiss.

In the cabbage garden

Martin Rattler stopped hoeing between the rows of cabbages, took out his (red-spotted, natürlich) handkerchief and mopped the perspiration that was running down his forehead and that he could feel gathering in his bushy eyebrows. What on earth was he going to do about this stupid promotion thing? Mary wanted him to prove to himself and to the railway that he was capable of being more than just a porter. Mary's mother, he suspected, while still wishing he could bring in more money to make life a bit easier for them all and to be able to put some aside to take care of the new baby's future, had an inkling that becoming a stationmaster would not necessarily suit him, and might prove difficult to undo if it should turn out to have been a mistake.

He seemingly lacked a competitive streak.

But he didn't want to let Jean down, and he didn't want to write himself off as being not up to the job. He went and sat down on the kitchen chair in the dappled shade of the cherry tree and began drawing a fish in the dusty soil with the toe of the old brown leather shoes he wore for gardening. Then he scuffed it out and tried to do a butterfly, but it looked more like a bumble bee. He lay back for a moment, meaning to go into the kitchen to get some cider, and looked up into the pink blossom. Something tumbled out of the tree and landed by his foot - a bee! he bent, gently scooped its motionless round furry body into a loose fold of his handkerchief, stood and carefully tipped it into a low-hanging cup of the pink petals. The bee came to life, scrambled round to face him, and very softly began to speak, seemingly talking to itself, in just the kind of warm, avuncular and slightly husky whisper you would expect from a bumble bee in that situation.

Here was this great lumbering, sweaty creature but with gentle hands and in clear internal distress about something. What could a middle-aged bombus do or say to be of service to it?

"All creatures have their appointed place and function..." is what the bee whispered to Martin.

Harold: Becoming a municipal Librarian

I wonder if I can do a sort of 2-tier narration dealing with the acquisition of Minic stuff through the internet/mail from Yorkshire, say, in the third person, and with the life within the Layout, say, in the first person and from the POV of, mainly, Martin. Course you can, Maurice!

Hang on a minute. Thinking about Olivia and Rex and how we don't actually know very much about even Rex (arguably a more important character than Olivia – but how can you say that, and what does it mean, if anything?), I wondered if I could have a letter from Rex to his mother. En route to that idea, and thinking about two of my characters getting married, I asked myself whether any of my characters is yet a sufficiently mature or rounded character to get married. And of course…

Bang! It hit me; what if Olivia is Rex's sister? Theologically, no doubt a heretical idea, though surely a harmless one, and it does feel as if it might conceal a deeper truth. Is there a way in which I can arrange for Max (or maybe Felix as his one-time agent on Earth) to be the brains behind the Layout? Jeez, do I have time to write this new novel that looks as though it is trying to get itself born here now? Answer: as the creator myself of The Novel, of course, I can do it. I just have to do it. Tie up the loose ends later in the rewrite.

One of Olivia's responsibilities is to arrange things so that the books people need to read will be available and, if necessary, fall at their feet at the appropriate moment, in the old derelict house, charity shop or library or even bookshop that they may just happen to visit. At least as far as that is possible (there are always alternative ways for the necessary ideas to come to them but – there being so many books about, to which most people pay no attention - the right book at the right time is often the easiest solution to achieve).

She really does, in her job go off at short notice to talk to people and fix things in far-off places.

Olivia has to turn up on the doorstep or be encountered casually down at the supermarket or the park or somewhere and get into conversation with Schneegwyn if she wants to help. Am I capable of writing that scene? Yes, of course I am. So do it.

A mysterious stranger

...emerges from the forest to save the lovely Schneegwyn...from mercenary loggers.

Names and stars

All these names with prominent final xes! – what can that signify, I ask myself: Max, Rex, Felix.

Rex's got to be almost incorruptible (though probably not a flywhisk-wielding Jainist). Kind of troubled and Hamlet-like about his mission to save/redeem (whatever that means) mankind. Rex is the non-executive branch of the family firm. Rex has nowadays progressed into something quite Sagittarian, but with depths that may suggest Scorpio. Traditionally Capricorn, though his mother maintains he is Aquarius.

Felix may be called whatever is the German word for plumtree (yes, it matters) actually Pflaumenbaum. Rethink this. Plumtree, spelled still, as in the earliest extant baptismal records from the 16th century parish church registers, Plumtre, suits Felix better.

Is Max a problem, astrologically? – Leo, I guess. And Sagittarius.

Olivia is the love interest for Rex, and the female interest/principle for Max. Olivia must be Aquarius.

Zoë Salt is the future, the ultimate, the yet-to-come. She is Yellow, the colour nearest to her Zed. So probably also Leo. She brings the sunshine wherever she goes, she can talk to anyone, she will talk to anyone, she talks to everyone. She lets them meet themselves and know themselves, perhaps for the first time. In her person, she is tawny as a lion or a lioness. She might almost have been an Yvonne, but her mother was Joy and named her with courage. Zo, Zozo and Zoetrope – she has been called by many names. Zoë. Life. The last word. She opens the doors.

Henrietta is a party girl. Does this mean she's a Gemini with Libra and maybe some Pisces in her chart? Oh, and deep down, Sagittarius.

Owen is largely Aries, but Otto seems to be possessed of a Taurus streak, too.

Schnee, Susan and possibly also Jean should be Cancerian, though Jean has a hefty dollop of something really sensible – could that be Capricorn? Or well-aspected Virgo?

I hate to think Martin is Scorpio, though hmm, he does seem not only obsessive but also secretive like Ben.

Felix is clearly ruled by Jupiter – Fish? - and also Venus - Bull? Libra?

Downey's Taurus plus, of course, Virgo in its policeman mood.

Olivia Vogel

If you were to find yourself through no fault of your own in deep trouble, the person you need on your case would be Olivia Vogel. Our Liv is a divinely authorized globetrotting troubleshooter with almost superpowers, and would have you sitting down at the big scrubbed kitchen table with a fresh pot of tea in no time - or would just quietly go out and shoot the person causing you grief. I hope you don't mind if I try writing you into a scene to find out how she handles it. I'll let you know if it's any good. And, of course, I'll change your name.

Max is the executive branch of Mundy, Mundy and Vogel – do I mean the executive branch? I mean CEO. It's Olivia Vogel who actually gets on the phone, gets on the bus (if she has to), gets in the car, gets on the train or the plane and sees that the right things happen, and I guess she might have the help of at least two assistants – Mike or Michelle and Gabriel or Gabrielle.

Ben on all the toy guns in the house

As kids we played at cowboys, we played at soldiers, we played at gangsters. So we always wanted to have guns.

First, at the age of four? Three? Dimly, in the days before school, a perfectly matched (that is to say, identical) pair of chromium plated "Gene Autrey" cowboy six-shooters in, I'm sure, holsters yet. It must have been 1947 at the latest – which I find hard to believe, because it feels as though the whole of the 1940s were The War – the Coastal Command book, my siren suit, that strange board game with the WAAFs, and the playing cards with Churchill, Hitler, Lord Gort and so on on them – and all before the street party for VE Day when Mrs Stone from across the road gave me that chunky stuffed Scotty dog made out of cassock material that I had for years. Still, when you're little, I suppose, an awful lot happens in a year, so the six-shooters could have appeared in 1947.

They were cap pistols. My Dad made for me out of soldered brass a holder for rolls of caps, a bit like two or three bottle tops attached to a backing plate that was meant to go on a belt alongside the holsters. I had that for years, too. I remember the revelation that cowboys had to have two or even three belts – one or two to have their pistol holster or holsters (the real star cowboys, the dangerous ones, had two guns) and one to keep their trousers up.

Somewhere in there, in my memory, was a rifle. We'd had pop guns, which were fun and worked with an efficient but stiff, I remember, pull-back action against a long, strong spring. But the cork they fired was supposed to be on a string (which was boring), which you could, of course, remove (for which you got told off because it was dangerous), and then you lost the cork. It was pretty well always Mum who would initiate a movement to tell us off for doing anything dangerous – usually with Dad as a sort of backup court of appeal. This is not the place to mention "wait till your father comes home" and the memory (that could be a false one) of being taken to bend over the dustbin in the garage and be walloped – satisfying word for a process that can only have been quite gentle – with a slipper. More of a show trial than a punishment.

There was another more serious toy rifle, a Winchester. It was a lever-action affair, as I recall – though I'm not clear whether cocking it meant it would fire a cork. I suppose it must have done; the capping mechanism would have been double-action, so to speak, operated by the trigger, and would surely not have required cocking.

When the "action", the mechanism, became detached through long hard use, it went on to be the mechanics of the submachine gun that by that time had become essential to my games. I should say our games, for even when Owen was not there to share and admire, there is always in my memories a sense of someone else being present. I can clearly remember making the wooden submachine gun and painting it matt battleship grey. There must have been a glut of films about "commando" types who no longer used rifles but submachine guns – Tommy guns or Stens – and the partisans or foreign allies would have their own ones with odd-shaped magazines. Mine, anyway was a straight magazine made from a chair leg and sticking out, I think at the side like the one on a Sten. There's been an attempt earlier (under the influence of Bevis…Aha! A whole new area opens up in my head. Bevis! At school we had a slim blue reading book, "Bevis and Mark," that we toiled through with some male teacher who has completely left my memory – unless it was the somewhat callow one who took me to the doctor's when I cut open my chin climbing along the school window ledges – another story entirely. Later, my sister Eva gave me a much fatter book: the full edition of "Bevis" which I loved.

Bevis and his inseparable sidekick Mark decide at some point to build a gun. So of course, I must have a go at doing likewise. We have Brown Bess as an example to guide us, hanging on the picture rail in the front room. Brown Bess is a percussion musket, as we call it, romantically imagined to be of English Civil War vintage but obviously not so as I now know – even if she originally had not a percussion lock but a flintlock as we fancied. She was usually to be found near the old black oak chest we called Elizabethan (indeed I think in the early years she lived inside it – probably till Dad and Mum thought it "safe" to hang her on the wall in full view), so gained antiquity by association. Antiquity and authenticity went hand-in-hand in our house and were held in high esteem. Hardly anything could be worse to our collective cultural snob mind than fake-ness, unless it was vulgarity or poor taste. The resulting firearm that I created actually looked vaguely oriental – not unlike some of the Arab rifles I saw on my visits to the Birmingham Museum and Art Gallery – because its stock was made from a section of interestingly curved mahogany that came from the back of a broken (but not, of course, discarded – we are talking here of my Dad) dining chair. The lock was from the aforementioned drop-action Winchester and the barrel was a piece of copper tube I can almost remember buying new (shock! horror! – no one in our family ever bought anything new) at the Ironmonger's. Or was that the barrel of my "Sten"? Whatever. Surely not both, though I did love copper for its pink colour and its amenableness to files and hacksaws. That would mean that at some point, we had an armoury of two firearms, so we could have fire-fights, me and Owen.

Not to mention the toy pistols to whose cataloguing I now return.

The pirate pistol. A double-barrelled cap pistol, almost certainly by the firm that my growing connoisseurship of the field was learning, was the most likely to produce acceptable weapons – despite the Lone*Star brand name having such by now lamentable associations with the cowboyishness I had grown out of in favour of Second World War games. There had been short-lived interest in a comic-book (what we would have called simply a 'comic') series about the Lone Star Ranger.

Very early on, I think, when I had been (briefly?) in the throes of having seen some film noir and "wanted to be" a spy character with a small, fairly flat and unobtrusive (but of course, nonetheless deadly) gun I could carry in the pocket of my notional lounge suit (small boys can entertain any number of patently untrue and mutually incompatible pieces of knowledge at the same time, even while going about a humdrum real life), I had acquired an "automatic," a small black jobbie with grips like match-strikers along the sides of what would in the real thing have been the cocking slide, and a solid trigger, that I cherished for a while but have a faint and regretful impression of having swapped away in exchange for what I cannot now remember. How I wish I had it still!

Then there was a bigger six-shooter, rather too showily chromium-plated for my taste, and with regretfully inauthentic bright red plastic grips, a spinning cylinder and loose plastic bullets in addition to the cap mechanism.(Well, I can't clearly visualize the mechanism now, but I assume it would have fired caps. I can't imagine anyone making one without it. It was nicely heavy, and the business (aha! It begins to come back to me now) of being able to take out and put back the bullets was a bonus. I rather fancy that the bullets were made to contain a single cap each, detonated as they came under the hammer, pretty much as in the real thing. Could that be true? If so, it would have come perilously close to almost being dangerous and even susceptible (in the hands of an ingenious child) to conversion into a working firearm. Which – after all – might have been what led us step-by-step to the pin-fire escapade.

There was also the Peacemaker – notable for its graceful lines (most "cowboy" guns in the shops were, to my snobbish museum-trained eye, pretty clunky design-wise, but this was a beauty, with smooth grips and a longer barrel than was usual) and a smooth cylinder.

Somewhere in there was also a fairly anonymous six-shooter that I worked on for a while to make it look more realistic. It was at the time in our life when Dad was working with pewter in his handicraft activities, and I was introduced to whatever chemical liquid it was that the pewter-working fraternity used to induce an oxidised "patina" to the otherwise shiny metal. Used to excess, this fluid would make many metals black, but diluted it merely turned the shiny "white metal" used by cap pistol makers into a not unconvincing dull grey that could be polished along the edges to simulate the wear of heavy use in combat.

For a while we would apply this treatment almost routinely to any newly acquired example of shoot'n iron almost as soon as it was out of its cellophane or box.

Then came the Luger (another from Lone*Star), and at last – we had longed for what seemed like years to have a fairly convincing British "service revolver" – there quietly appeared on the market (and I don't know why it didn't occur to us to start buying them in multiples, or at least to get two while we were in the toyshop) a pretty authentic-looking Webley. A little on the small side, but so close to right that I added it to the collection without hesitation. Just a shame that it appeared rather late in the day, when we were really getting a bit too old to be playing with guns in quite the way we had for years.

Which I suppose (unless some other firearm has slipped my memory along the way) brings me to what I might call the late phase. Starting with Venice, and with counselling.

Tinnitus

A sound like metallic running water, or dead leaves blowing about in an empty schoolyard. And at night, it sounded like a fire burning.

Early days – evolving landscape forms: long-nosed mountain

Olivia this morning is in her working outfit of a voluminous longish skirt, loose-fitting top and soft boots. In the big upstairs room above the office, she swoops around the table that is the temporary home for the section of the landscape she is working on with her Stanley knife in hand, making yard-long sweeping cuts in the thick cardboard that forms the foundation ground level of the model. She lifts a section of the board she has cut and glues a block of wood under it, instantly creating a valley in the grey hillside. Already, a row of buildings she constructed yesterday evening from white, grey and dull blue card is waiting on a shelf, ready to take its place alongside the combe.

Ready to hand is a box full of broken chunks of white polystyrene, liberated from the doorway of the television and audio shop two doors away, which will become rocky outcrops before the morning is much older. She pauses to glance again at the series of photos, sketches and plans that are pinned up on the long wall behind her before turning back to draw in pencil the line a pathway must take as it rises up the slope from the building platform.

Some dolls are more rigid

From having to look after her plainer, more anxious older sister Margot, the pretty Henrietta had developed a rather truculent and self-pitying manner that didn't sit well with her aquamarine eyes and golden curls.

All three of the bedroom dressing-table dolls had a right strop going on this morning – well, not Zoë. She's always cheerful and eager-looking – but the others, Hen and Margot, both looked dazed as if they had been awake half the night, grumpy and despondent. To be fair, Margot does usually look as if she is miles away, but Hen is moody, and since she got tipped over the other morning when Mrs Thing moved the tea tray, and was sat up straight again, she hasn't seemed right.

Henrietta loves a party, gets on well with Zoë and puts up with Margot because she's her sister, though sometimes a bit of a pain, and she fears Margot may never really grow up into a fully rounded person – but she may surprise her.

(There's no reason, by the way, why I have to say what the relationship is between the three girls. I'm not sure whether a reader would find it intolerable or even irritating to not have it spelled out. I will need to take advice on this question.)

So, all the same, I ask Margot the question: Margot, can you tell me who you three girls are?

Margot says, "Henrietta is my big sister. She looks after me when my Mummy is not here. Zozo might be my other sister – only she might have a different Daddy. I'm nine, Zozo is ten, and Henny Penny is eleven."

I ask Zoë. She doesn't want to say because she is not absolutely certain. She thinks her Dad is Ludwig. Margot has the ages right. Zoë could be Jean's younger sister, which would mean Susan is her mother. Character-wise, this would seem to make sense. Ludwig is not Hen's father.

Nigel Harrison

My Dad and my Mum, and my stuff. I don't care if people don't like me. What do they know? Wankers.

Coin soldiers

Ludwig Swanning is playing with coins from his Mama's purse - she is showing him the portraits of his uncles, grandparents and cousins on the coins. He is more interested in the patterns that magically happen when he lays out rows and columns of the little coins on his grandfather's map table like soldiers on parade in blocks and columns four abreast, eight abreast, marching into battle or to their valiant deaths at his command – formations of men silver or gold or copper or bronze turning and wheeling - hexagons suddenly appear...Packing the men as closely as he can (but with enough space to draw a sword though not to present a carbine or musket - no, the foot soldiers have no carbines: carbines are the arms issue to the mounted scouts – les francs-tireurs; the freelances)...the boy grows restless and bored, goes in search of his Uncle Otto for a game of draughts or possibly Oxo.

Prudence and George

I think we assumed the old broken tiles that Ben dug up from the garden in his archaeological excavation phase had been laid down by previous owners as garden paths. But they could have been the remains of previous houses that had existed on the site long before the building of the development we lived in.

"I wonder what he thinks he's doing out there in the flower border. Seems to be burying things or digging things up. I do hope it's not going to be archaeology again. The paths still haven't recovered from the last excavations, have they? I keep finding little holes where he's dug out broken bits of those tiles he found. Made a mess all over the place. I know it's important to let him feel the garden is his as well as ours, and I suppose I'd hate it if he just stuffed in his room all day with his nose in a book or something – I almost was afraid that was going to happen with his sister, though girls tend to be a bit different. Yes, even Zozo has a ladylike side to her - and I would hate to interfere and say he's not to make a mess. That'd be dreadfully hard for him – no hope of that anyway, since he's your son - but I just hope the garden will recover at some point, before too long. Oh, look, he has made a little staircase going down. Isn't that clever! I wonder what it's meant to be for. Is he burying toy soldiers? You don't think he's been upset by all this Poppy Day stuff, do you, and the Remembrance Day parade? Maybe we should have left him at home. That would have been a shame, though – he was so much enjoying himself marching along by the side of the band. And I was so proud of the way he stood so quiet and still when the other boys were larking about taking the mickey out of the Home Guard sergeant-major during the speeches and the two minutes silence. I wonder if it's time to see about him joining the Boy Scouts."

IV

Olivia's Workroom

My workroom, two floors up in the building that housed the Mundy offices, was between a storeroom full of old plans and a green-painted door labelled *PATERNOSTER ACCESS TO UE: mind the gap.*

At the Palace

The cavernous kitchen of the palace, with its shelves and shelves of pots and pans and copper jelly moulds of every imaginable size and extravagant shape, is where the boy learns that people have masses of things that they don't need. But also that he is an important little person and will be indulged.

She calls him Louis rather than Ludwig (the French are so much more refined) but also *Mein Kleiner Luftmensch* – mainly to annoy her brother Otto.

The Three Towns

There are three towns here set in a sort of enchanted triangle.

SEAGLASS

The crazy, funky town of the curtain tells you the answer is behind the veil, in the spirit - the spiritual. Here you can do Tarot, buy crystals, beat a shaman's drum. In my book you can also visit the seaside, sprawl dozing on a bacon-striped deckchair, meditate and suck rock. It's a heart town, a water town, finally a fire and water town.

FUSSEL DARCY

The shambolic town of the death of capitalism will sell you practically everything you need. It's where the sheep and the cheese and the cider apples used to come to market. It looks after your sick body in its hospitals and tells you the answer is in the here and now. It's a dirty old earth town.

SPRINGTON

You do your banking in the shiny town of ideas that calls itself a city. Books, music, religion, schools. It is certain the answer is in the mind, in the head. This is the town where history is written down, an air town. It's, in many ways, a gateway and sometimes a suburb of Rome.

All three are barmy towns, crazy towns, lovely towns. Seaglass is the craziest, with an abbey and at least two churches, thinks itself the centre of the universe and is widely known for its joss-stick-scented High Street full of crystal shops and hippie weirdo bookshops and witchcrafty Taroty brass bell and bowl and candle shops with incense wafting out of every door. Like Totnes, it doubtless has more healers per head of population than clients for them to heal.

Saddest of the three is Fussel Darcy, which seems to be trying yet again to ban the out-of-work ciderheads from the Market Cross and pull itself up by its bootstraps. A century or more ago it was a thriving sheep market town; now it has a cider factory and a prison, a touch-and-go theatre school and still too many pubs. A big Tesco has killed off the high street shops and the place is defiant but struggling to maintain some kind of community heartbeat.

Springton, with a couple of famous schools and a tiny family-run multi-screen 'club' cinema, is more confident. Secure in its sense of its own importance. It doesn't have to struggle to keep the tourists coming to photograph the cathedral and the Bishop's palace. But the people are just weird in a different way, with classier accents and more old money.

The imagined presence of a nearby nursing home is an excuse for a reasonably healthy local passenger service... and its continuing existence through and beyond the Beeching era. A fictional quarry not far away adds significant volume to the national freight traffic on the line.

There's a relaxed attitude about the area. If a carpet-fitter or a home-call hairdresser says he or she'll get back to you tomorrow, you don't actually wait in. And if a car is being driven too fast, it's not likely to be a local. As if to say What's the rush? There could be a gurt tractor or a herd of Holstein milkers in the road. Next week will do just as well.

The Original Princess Schneegwyn From 'Way Back

Let's see if we can clarify the Princess Schneegwyn situation. It was a time of magic and a land of myth. She was never Cinderella (though we just might want to squeeze in a reference to La Cenerentola somewhere for the sake of being pretentious). She was Snow White in that she was carried off from the dangerous jealous stepmother/witch situation in her "village" (but princesses come from something grander than a village, so it's got to be instead a place with a castle. Read chateau – but maybe one of those run-down, fallen-on-hard-times ones, like Baron Hardup's town house in Cinderella) by a handsome and reasonably charming prince (Ludwig) to go and live with him – not in a palace because he is acting without his father the King's blessing – in a quite humble place deep in the forest.

Kullervo seized the girl and pushed her under the rugs of his sleigh (in the Finnish Kalevala) and saved her from tyranny (the Russian monolith).

Do we want a desertion and "all men are bastards" theme here? If so, the prince will obviously have to run off and leave her to cope on her own. Or maybe, just maybe, mother-in-law will reveal herself to be an absolute brick and give support. The amber mine turns out to be her financial salvation. Present this as the myth of the founding of the town and estate of Bernstein, and the "present day" amber heiress millionairess Princess Schneegwyn as the jokingly so called "reincarnation" of the mythical princess of the same name. Princess Priceless. I think a female line of succession and inheritance is called for as local custom.

The Owl Tea Cosy And The Dolls

A tea cosy in the form of an owl – rather stylishly worked in patchwork, with pleasing paisley elements and brown buttons for eyes (which I guess gives him a unique outlook) – sat on the tea tray on the bedroom chest of drawers, alongside the three dolls, Henrietta, Margot and Zoë seated on a box of tissues like three wise monkeys. I'm not sure how acceptable this kind of whimsy will be, but I fancy expressing how the owl sees the world. He has a pessimistic expression that suggests a certain jaundicedness – which would make him a suitable ally for Margot when she's in danger of being overpowered or outvoted by the two more cheerful others. The three dolls will certainly have a say in the story, and may indeed become real people.

Because there are three dolls, there will always be two opinions about each of them, held by people who do not know what it feels like to be them. And however compassionate all of them may be, each will in some way prefer one of the other two to the third one.

Well-meaning friends...

... would sometimes give Olivia figures that were in the wrong scale. Such as that silly big donkey she eventually grew quite attached to and couldn't bring herself to throw away.

Platform

"The people gathered, more to see Otto's impressive new and surprisingly white moustaches than anything else, when the train brought him back to his native town after he had completed his studies away at military college. But they were there all the same."

Can it be that, when the villagers crowd the platform to meet Otto's train, among the people who get off is Owen, Ben's Welsh friend, and the person Owen sees on the platform is Schneegwyn looking irresistible in a white duffel coat? And is it possible that they will go together to the Schloss Hotel? What will happen there, I wonder. Perhaps there will be a body? Perhaps a ransom note…

She was so excited she wanted to jump up and down, but she was holding her suitcase in one hand and her overnight bag in the other, so she just gave a little jiggle as she walked across the reception lobby with its marble tiled floor

He (who?) idolised his Maman qua the Bugatti Queen

Dressed from head to toe in white leather, or sometimes pale green (what she referred to as her "buff"), she would be carried along shoulder-high by admiring crowds after racing first to the finishing line yet again in her trade-mark Bugatti, blue as the Virgin's robe in some Renaissance altar-piece. It seemed she was on the front page of newspapers almost every week in that jazzy Art Deco period when her fame was at its peak, photographed in Paris, Monte Carlo, St Tropez.

    His own car was sky-blue rather than that lapis lazuli (lovely name for a pigment), and as he drove it through the twists and turns of the dusty empty roads between Rome and the coast, he was in his mind re-living the world of the nineteen-twenties' and thirties' motoring posters that adorned the walls of the flat where he had lived with her – racing-cars' wheels at crazy angles and in exaggerated perspective scattering geese at the roadside while tanned and white-teethed peasants grinned in amazement, encouragement, collusion or alarm.

A false start

It is as if there is a school staff room. The headmaster, of course, would be Max, who would have his own office and spend little time here with the other teachers, who would include: Eric Downey, history teacher; Olivia Vogel, some kind of house mistress but also an art teacher. Otto probably got a job as a sports teacher but also taught maths, and Harold, being pedantic by nature, would be teaching English. Susan Marshwood would teach needlework.

The Princess thing

I/we need to look again at this whole Princess thing – think about it in the light of all the above, but also of the symmetrical-faced pretty girl in the Bay restaurant with the downcast and slightly hooded eyes, who could have stepped out of a late medieval portrait and who moves her eyes rather more than her head (she could be 14: she could at a pinch be 21. There was at first a young man with a dog and a child at the table with her – initially I assumed that she and the child were sisters, but she could have been the young mother).

Ben on the real guns

There were other real guns in the house, apart from Brown Bess. We knew that, but we didn't know where they were kept hidden. Or, actually, how many there might have been. I'm sure we asked Dad, but he would have been evasive on the subject. At some point, the great heavy old Gasser revolver came out of hiding, and I was even allowed to take it with me to school one day when we all were supposed to take in an interesting object for a display. I remember (I think) Dad carefully sawing off the tip of the firing pin from the hammer to make it safe, and one of the male teachers trying to show off his familiarity with guns by handling it with none of the awed respect the rest of us showed. It was an ancient-looking relic of a thing, brown with rust despite being normally kept wrapped up in a dried-out oily rag. What plating there may once have been had almost all disappeared, the horn plates on the grip were cracked and stained like an old cigarette-holder and there was no ammunition for it. How Dad came by it we were never told. Eventually I did do a bit of research – in fact I think I must have asked some kind of dealer about it – doubtless during one of the many adult periods when I was short of money – which was when I learned that it was called a Gasser (and a close inspection did reveal that name engraved somewhere on the frame).

But when we were kids, heck, it was a real gun and we were excited to be able to mess about with it, wondering at its weight and clumsiness. How on earth did spies and gangsters manage to go about their spying and gangstering business, lumping a great heavy bulky chunk of metal like that in their pockets? We tried carrying it in our school blazer pockets – impossible, and it threatened to fall out and bruise someone's foot.

But there was, we knew, another revolver. It was probably kept up in the loft – a place difficult to get to, access involving standing on a chair on the landing at the top of the stairs, pushing the trap-door open and climbing in – then realizing you needed a torch and could only walk on the bits that had floorboards, otherwise your foot would break through the plaster. So we didn't go up there. But from time to time we had a feeling that the weapon might have been moved to Dad's Box. At various times there were two Dad's Boxes. One was a big yellow boxwood tool chest that usually lived in an inaccessible part of The Shed. It would appear when a particular fairly precious tool was required – such as the tapping thingies to make a screw thread. We kind of thought that sometimes The Gun might have been kept in there – or its tin of ammunition might. But there was another Dad's Box – a Chinese lacquer jobby that we thought was kept in the bottom of Dad's wardrobe. Not somewhere we went.

Eventually though, in the nature of things, as we grew older and more daring and were more often (not often) left alone in the house with time on our hands, we found it. And the little tin box with the rounds in. [do you know, I suspect that Mom and Dad must have sometimes used the lock on their bedroom door? We kids were never allowed to lock our bedroom doors – that would have been asking for trouble and too dangerous, though I'm sure my two sisters at least must have at various times longed to be able to do just that]

It was quite a lovely thing, blued steel – smaller and quite delicate compared to the old Gasser. Dad had acquired it, we were told, for Mom when he went away to France in the RAF – though the word was that she hated it and would never have used it even if the Germans had arrived and she had had to defend her honour.

Unbeknown to us, it later turned out that there had been a third pistol somewhere about the place. Uncle Walter's service revolver from the Boer War. A dinky little nickel-plated Webley that he would apparently have bought for himself from an officer's outfitter before embarking for South Africa.

Fixing the period

In Britain, Queen Anne's on the throne, so it must be the early eighteenth century. Fine houses with hipped roofs, a war going on all over the continent. I think in the book she will not die in 1714 as history books would have it. I need some kind of marker to define the style and feel of the period - and the 18th century seemed to go on for ever. For heaven's sake, it reached almost all the way to Queen Victoria. Apart from 1066, Magna Carta and the Civil War, almost everything important seemed to happen in the 18th century. And on the Continent.

A good thing Dr Downey can't overhear these thoughts! He would be appalled by my playing fast and loose with the 'facts' of history.

Mental note to self: define frock coat (look up Pepys' suits).

Two dolls

Nothing happens. Let's see if we can bring to life, breathe life into, these 'poor' 'orphaned' dolls with their frozen half-smiles. They just sit and stand there, but they exude their stories. Hen and Zo both go through life with their eyes wide open, though they see different things. Hen sees a world of men and dresses and parties: Zo sees a world of troubled people, each fighting their own secret battles. Hen misses her Mum: Zo misses her Dad, though she only remembers him as someone who would turn up with a book or two from time to time. She needs to become (is becoming) the superhero of her own movie.

Life on the Layout

Martin had spent a week, he thought, carefully hoeing between the cabbage rows. For a while he was put in charge of a gang of men doing something with ballast and shovels and having to scramble up the embankment out of danger whenever a train was coming. Then one day he had found himself standing leaning on a five-bar gate alongside the shiny dark red Humber Super Snipe, in a part of the Layout he hadn't often seen. He fancied he felt there was an expectant sort of atmosphere in the air – as if there was some task he was supposed to perform – and yet he had no idea of what that task might be. Maybe he was meant to be just paying attention, observing every detail of where he was and what he could see, and maybe the thoughts that went through his head…well, the ground seemed very dry and hard underfoot. The sky is kind of hazy, but it's a bright day - we seem to be enjoying a long spell of this sort of weather – and there's no wind to speak of. In fact this doesn't seem to be a windy part of the world at all. You hardly ever see the trees moving in the slightest… Hello – that's new…

Yes, I'm a secret agent. Who said that?

When you walk round the corner, out of my sight, you leave my universe and continue in your own.

Martin may also have the Spy complex – but in his case because he keeps finding himself standing about in parts of the Layout where he has never been before, with no real business to be there. [this may be because the minute the operator/designer/ controller lays hands on him to whiz him through the air, he goes blank till his feet are back on solid baseboard or whatever.] He may be the one whose friends (if he has any: wife and mother in law if not) think he may be a spy.

This is NOT the same as, for instance, Max becoming the consciousness of Felix.

Designing soldiers

Sitting in front of the looking glass at mid-day I looked at my face, and noticed my eyes, as violet as the light in the meadow behind the palace, there in the palace district.

This diary that you gave me, dear Mama, will be a work of art – either that or a confessional. Or a tissue of lies.

I'm sorry if I frightened the chambermaids.

In the Smaller Library, Ludwig and one of his generals were sitting with regimental tailors' pattern books open on the table in front of them – page after hand-coloured page of waistcoats and intricately-shaped pattern pieces in red, royal blue, yellow, white, grey, pale blue; and elaborate knots, epaulettes and froggings of gold braid, and an index of row upon row of tiny soldiers, drummers and trumpeters at attention in a bewildering array of plain or fancy dress - "Yes, ah yes, my soldiers must be beautiful. I can see it now – their (what are their hats called – shakos?) – their shakos shining in the spring sunshine."

"Sir, the tailors report they are having difficulty getting enough brown bear skins. Could we possibly allow some of the mounted infantry to have black shakos? We have a warehouse full of the black bear skins."

"What, and look like British Grenadiers? Certainly not. I am seeing brown fur shakos to match their pretty brown boots. The hunters must work harder. Send them further into the forest. And of course not all of them wear shakos. Do you think I know nothing? Let me remind you I have been studying these matters since before I could read. Some will have those glorious tall hats shaped like fish, with the golden plates on the front glinting, like so many bishops' mitres – can you not see it? A whole regiment of tall bishops marching and counter-marching" The boy clapped his hands with excited pleasure. Grandmama Esterházy will be so pleased – she loves to watch them countermarching – just like a piece of live weaving being woven down there in the square. And I want them to have numbers painted on the golden fronts of their mitres, so that I can look through my spy-glass and see if they are carrying out the drill correctly."

"Yes, of course, your highness. Er, that would be brass, of course, not actual gold," the tailor ventured, thinking of his annual estimates. "The men would polish them to look like gold. Or they could be gilt."

"Yes, yes, so long as it shines. You must give an order that they are to have time for polishing. And the equipment – mind you do not stint on brushes and rags and powdered brick for the hats. And now we must also consider something for the winter. Yes, a different regiment. The winter is a splendid opportunity. They will be able to have especially shiny boots – tall ones against the mud and the snow. How I love to see the brown mud churned up on a winter march, like chocolate against the white of the snow. And to wear in the snow, I think the pale blue tunics we discussed earlier. Where are they – ah here, look. With the white reveres and for these, I think, the silver buttons instead of the gold. So they will have to be issued with – what do you call them? – those clever little leather cards with the slots in so they can polish their silver buttons without soiling the white buckram. Do I mean buckskin, or buckram?"

"Buckram, yes, Sir, pipe-clayed, it will be."

Bullfinches, chaffinches, blue tits, the black and white and red greater spotted woodpecker and particularly the goldfinch, are quite reminiscent of regimental dress in the James Laver book, what with their scarlet tufted headgear, their black-and-yellow patterned coat-tails and the white side-flashes on their drabber winter-issue greatcoats.

Scale

For North America the National Model Railroad Association (NMRA) standard S-1.2 defines HO scale 3.5 mm (0.1378 in) as representing 1 real foot (304.8 mm) - a ratio of 1:87.0857142, usually rounded to 1:87.1. The precise definition of HO or H0 scale varies slightly by country and manufacturer.

HO is the most popular model railroad scale in both continental Europe and North America, whereas OO scale (4 mm:foot or 1:76.2 with 16.5 mm track) is still dominant in Britain. There are some modellers in Great Britain who use HO scale, and the British 1:87 Scale Society was formed in 1994.

O scale (or O gauge) is a scale commonly used for toy trains and rail transport modelling. Originally introduced by German toy manufacturer Märklin around 1900, by the 1930s three-rail alternating-current O gauge was the most common model railroad scale in the United States and remained so until the early 1960s. In Europe, its popularity declined before World War II due to the introduction of smaller scales.

V

Schnee at the mirror

Princess Schnee is a bit obsessed, understandably, about genes she'd inherited – for fullness and brownness of hair but also for comparatively early onset of poor eyesight, deafness and poor memory.

Schnee sings "the moment I wake up/before I put on my make up" to her looking glass. She is, of course, not only Snow White – step-daughter of the wicked queen (and therefore might be concerned to be in some sense the fairest of them all) – but also probably Susan's mother or grandmother.

The map in the hotel room revealed just how unbelievably extensive the Mitteleuropawald had been. And yet within that deep dark, almost unbroken expanse (stretching right across the map from - what - Belgium? Yes, probably Belgium, to the Caucasus) of mile after square mile of dense trees, the map showed no centre of population larger than a small town. Alongside it on the wall a second, more colourful map showed a patchwork of dukedoms, principalities and tiny kingdoms owned and ruled by a scattering of little local Dukes, minor Kings and Princes.

There had been families living for generations in what she thought of as genuinely "fairy tale" conditions – whole families living and sleeping together in what were basically single-roomed, probably turf-thatched cottages – as often as not sharing the space at night with a cow or a pig, grandmothers living alone in isolated hovels, helpful woodsmen, if you were lucky, passing by every few days at most, bears and wolves of course in those days, no doubt evil stepmothers (stepmothers were by definition almost always evil – ex officio, as they say), avaricious millers, probably dwarves – not to mention assorted mis-shapen cripples and psychopaths, little local tyrants, no doubt wicked uncles, and probably also witches who may or may not have really fattened up for food any children they came across. It was actually reminiscent of what even present day existence is apparently like in those backwoods hillbilly areas of the U.S.A. where you sometimes hear dreadful stories of children locked in a room for the whole of their childhood, tied to a table or a bed and as like as not really abused by some parent or relative.

No wonder the Victorians, was it, were so horrified by what they thought were the lurid imaginings of Hans Andersen and the Brothers Grimm. Though I bet there were thousands of tales to be told in Victorian London about kids living with the most appalling abuse – you get a glimpse of it in Dickens, don't you, if you read between the lines of the sentimental tosh parts.

When Downey met Olivia

Downey first encountered Olivia at one of the annual model railway exhibitions held in Springton, where she had gone with her son, Andrew. She was squatting down with her head at the boy's shoulder, sharing his rapt delight at the trains' movements and becoming immersed in her own wonder at the lifelike details of a modelled stretch of trackside landscape - cottage back gardens looking like allotments, running down to the railway line, with a tiny figure in an apron, frozen for ever in the act of pegging out tiny washing on an almost invisible clothesline.

As Olivia straightened and turned to move along with the boy to another part of the crowded exhibition, she beamed at Downey waiting to move into the space she was vacating, and her infectious grin swept over him like a warm searchlight. He thought in that moment that this tall brown-haired young woman enjoying a day with her son was the most beautiful person he had ever seen.

What bothered Downey (and Andrew too) was that the wonderful scale detailing that gave many of the model layouts on show their realism was so often spoiled by the clumsiness of the fences. Gazing engrossed and lost in the miniature world was so enjoyable, until one spotted a field of convincing cows or horses grazing a grassy slope alongside the railway tracks, and the illusion was ruined by a row of wonky fence posts strung with impossibly thick wire.

Later that day at the café, Olivia wouldn't let Downey pay for her coffee.

Henrietta tells the tale

"In the olden time before this," began Hen, "in the mysterious days when those electric batteries were made in clay pots that the archaeologists have found that are older than Babylon, and when in far-off India they had made steel posts that still survive and have not corroded – despite having been made long, long before in the West men had discovered how to refine even pig-iron – in those days, in a great green secret valley where the borders of Poland used to meet the wild woods of Carpathia, a wilderness of amber-weeping trees concealed the kingdom of Schneegwyn the snow-white princess and her children the tiny miners."

Margot's flat brown eyes had glazed over as she gazed into the distance and saw it all. She sat between her two cousins not speaking, anxious already about what dreadful history might be about to be unfolded.

"A dire plague had emptied her village, so that the place that once was full of a noisy bustle of blacksmiths and travelling merchants and farmers trying to sell their cows was nowhere to be found, and all that remains is a big field full of green lumps and bumps and when the wind is right there is a whispering of ghosts in a tongue no-one any longer understands."

"Tell us more about Schneegwyn," said Zoë, who was too new to have heard any of this rigmarole before, and was eager for any information about the family that had adopted her. "Why did she need tiny miners?"

"Great-grandfather Otto's ancestors came from such a town – if you could call it a town," continued Hen, ignoring the question. "When he went away to Germany to learn be a general, he would have had to travel on the carrier's cart, because trains had not yet been invented."

"And I know great-grandfather Otto had big white moustaches when he came back from the Low Countries. I have seen it in the picture of him in the residents' lounge. Did he get his white hair from Schneegwyn? Was he her son?" asked Zoë.

"Zozo, Zozo, don't get so impatient," said Henrietta, "I was telling you about how Schneegwyn came to live in the forest. She had been carried away there when she was young and beautiful by the charming Prince Ludwig – who had not even heard of the great plague or the lost village…

"Ludwig who had the toy soldiers," interrupted Margot, remembering that story she had heard.

Henrietta laughed her tinkly golden laugh. "Ludwig had real solders, too – great regiments and armies of them – but he treated them like his toy soldiers. Marched them up and down all day and would not let them do any fighting to spoil their smart uniforms. But I'm sure that was after he had left Schneegwyn and gone back to his kingdom in the mountains. Or was it before he met Schnee – while he was still a really young man, not more than a teenager even?"

Tikkun olam

Jews believe that the performing of ritual *mitzvoth* (good deeds, commandments, or religious obligations) is a means of *tikkun olam,* helping to perfect the world, and that the performance of more *mitzvoth* will hasten the coming of the Messiah. This belief dates back at least to the early Talmudic period. According to Rabbi Yochanan, quoting Rabbi Shim'on bar Yochai, the Jewish people will be redeemed when every Jew observes Shabbat (the Sabbath) twice in all its details. This suggests that *tikkun olam* will prove successful with the coming of the Messianic Age.

In George's diary: Despite my many faults and failings and the one or two dreadful pieces of selfishness and poor judgement, about which I don't intend to tell you, dear Reader, I seem to be a likeable enough person. Pretty harmless, you'd think.

As a young man, I suppose I intended to become a better person one day but, unless I knew how to do that, I imagine I didn't think of searching out ways to achieve it, and left it to sort itself out. Gradually the intention would have faded away.

French landscape models

Max had learned from ancient experiences to resist the temptation to interfere in human affairs as far as he could... but he did arrange for Olivia to visit in the cellars under the Louvre the great suite of models of the French countryside that King Louis the Fourteenth had made at the time when he was occupied with war against the Dutch.

Can you imagine a "hands-off" deity? It really is the only sensible approach to managing a planet and its denizens. For the first few million years, he had been content to sit back and watch as the processes he had set in motion worked themselves out - in retrospect the time has passed like a couple of days. But then the language problem had arisen, people started working together in groups and then the idea of national identities surfaced, and then attempts at empire-building, and then war had become a bit of a habit over growing areas of the globe.

The road system

Oh, man, this is almost as frustrating as living in the real world. And I got into making the layout to escape from the real world into a world I could control. We could call the town Fallerton – at least for now. The system allows us to have some inclines but, as on what you might call real roads, the gradients don't need to be too steep or else the available vehicles will lack the power to get up the hills or over the bridges.

You see Faller roadways on exhibition layouts, but when you come to build one into your own layout you find how expensive the vehicles are and that they usually only work if the road surface is absolutely smooth and level. Not happy with any kind of scenic detailing that interferes with that. And it's hard to find any other vehicles than big square buses and coaches and heavy trucks. The tool for cutting the groove to take the guide wires is okay to use but all the curves need to be pretty smooth and with large radiuses for instance. Not much scope for messy realism.

Here, in a calmer corner of Otto's mind...

Otto's adult plan for an Almost Torpedo (*Beinahetorpedo*) depended on the use of a perpetual motion motor and so was a failure, but the idea was in some way interesting – a couple of sealed aluminium cylinders pointed at each end (can you picture them?) provide the buoyancy. It was to have had (but had not) some way of distinguishing between English and German warship targets (or indeed any other nationality). The device was to be simply released towards an enemy fleet by a secret agent and left to blow up whatever vessel it first bumped into. What you might truly call hit and miss, but strangely, the idea does seem to have been taken seriously by the German navy for a while. You will find a note later in this narrative about a different, model, submarine he had made in his boyhood from a short-length of broomstave.

Rex: Bugatti

Great car, that Bugatti. Got me from Anzio home to the Rome flat in less than three hours after my spin down to the coast. Wind in my ears, all that. Always tempting, these late summer days, these empty lanes, all this time on my hands. Takes my mind off Olivia. Dreamed about her again last night. Pity she has to be stuck in Head Office. We could make a great team. I suppose we do make a great team, but you know what I mean. Long distance on the phone is no substitute for having a real warm, funny, gorgeous-looking girl here with me in the car. What a looker! Thank God she's finally shot of that useless Andy. Plonker.

His copy of the glossy Bugatti owners' magazine had come in the post that morning, inspiring him to put on his brown leather Biggles helmet and goggles, unlock the garage and take his partly-restored Bugatti for a spin, scattering chickens and geese, along the Italian autumn lanes to the seaside.

Europe from the air

When whoever it is goes to Bernstein – as it might be for a TV programme about tracing their family tree and researching the amber industry – he or she will become aware from the plane of the great surviving expanse of the Great European Forest stretching for much of the time from horizon to horizon below them.

Not many travellers came along the road through the forest in those days, but the town market occasionally buzzed with excitement when an itinerant merchant or cobbler or knife-grinder brought word to the villages hidden among the trees, about barely credible experiments being carried out in Vienna, Danzig or far-off Moscow, that apparently had created light from something called electricity, so that candles and oil lamps would no longer be called for. Here in the village, for Heaven's sake, even steam power was hardly ever thought about. Horses or water mills gave any power that was needed over and above what might be got from a couple of strong men's arms and backs. That's how it had been here for as long as anyone could remember – since the time when the Roman legions turned back from the edge of the dense dark expanse of trees that seemed to have nothing to offer that might be of use to their empire and worth the risk of ambush by locals.

One-take Rosario, the happy man

Rosario is lucky. He is popular with film audiences because he is almost always cast as a calm, relaxed and charming character. Directors like him and call him "One-take" because he listens to what they say, doesn't argue, learns his lines, turns up sober and on time and doesn't trip over the furniture on set. Although he is not physically large, he has a powerful screen presence, exuding a quiet strength that more flamboyant actors enjoy playing off. So he is making good money but is content to live quite modestly and stay out of the papers. He accepts any role he is offered and goes home after each shoot to a simple apartment in a quiet unremarkable street.

He acts as if his Dad were chief of police - he lets nothing bother him. His one extravagance is his car. He only has the one, a deceptively ordinary-looking body that was hand-built for him to conceal a powerful engine and has exceptional handling.

Ben's Dad on pistols

I sometimes wonder whether we should maybe not have given him that first pair of Gene Autry cap pistols – as if we might have started something that was better not started.

This journal belongs to Margot

I think I'm catching a cold. Hen will look after me. I hate wearing black. I just have to keep reminding myself there is only this endless moment, and hold tight onto Henrietta.

Today I have been good and quiet. I did not get excited or upset when we had a new sister. I think she is my cousin. She is called Zozo and she stands up (we sit down). She is where I was, nearest the bedroom door. She is nice. Hen was telling us a fairy tale…

Downey can't cope

Eric Downey is wide awake at three in the morning with the light on. He is trying to make a chart, to help him get a handle on history and what happened when. And where. How does J. S. Bach, for instance, relate to Queen Anne, and the Hundred Years' War?

On the floor of his room he has spread out his big sheet of paper as if it were a map of the world. Along the top are the centuries, and down the side he can't decide whether to put the places or the categories – war, science, art and music and so on. He is sure he has seen in some book or other such a chart, but he suspects it was only a small, partial one detailing events in a single country or a single area of activity. The idea is growing on him that he needs a third dimension, to somehow incorporate another layer of information – either that or else produce a series of charts: say one for each century, or one for each country, perhaps. But that would fail to show the links through time that he is trying to clarify. Even if he limits himself to Europe, the task seems impossible, but Eric is not one to admit defeat without a struggle. Never give up, never give in, as his Mum used to chant to him when he was a boy.

1959

A film "Europe from the Air", revealing patterns unsuspected and beautiful as abstract paintings. Nicholas de Stael died that year (or was it 1950 the tall Russian painter threw himself from a high place in Paris?) A packet of black and white photographs 3 inches square or smaller – one shows a little crowd, a group, of maybe a hundred of those red roadworks lamps you don't see anymore since Tildawn dominated the market with their yellow battery jobbies. These were I suspect paraffin ones, shaped like little plump phone boxes with a curl of a handle on top to hang them by, and four round glass eyes - a little alien army lurking at a corner as if waiting to cross a busy road or take over the town.

Those were the days when men going to work in pinstripe suits would also wear a bowler hat, when The Boss in any office was treated with respect and probably addressed as "Sir", that end-of-an-era time just before mini-skirts and the Beatles and Woodstock in America, before young people had money in their pockets and the Pill.

His first job, and he was meeting people like him who worked in Birmingham city centre, who had money of their own for the first time. His first pay packet. He went to the Rag Market, chose himself a square yard of a couple of colourful fabric designs that excited him, took them home and hung them on the wall of his room. Got a camera (this was the era of Blow-Up, David Hemmings, David

Bailey); a Dansette.

I remember my friend Harold saying there's nothing so dreadful as old librarians, or even readers, who feel it is their duty to write a novel or other kind of book as a way of "giving something back" to the world they once were part of and enchanted by. What's dreadful is that they can from time to time see on a shelf in their mind's eye any number of long forgotten books that they once read or indeed only handled in passing, and will seek them out, look them up, endlessly go round in the circle of buying again and giving away or losing copies, looking always in those books for something that was never there but was in their life at the time they first encountered them. Only really good old librarians, those who treat books as simple products or commodities, are exempt from this kind of behaviour.

VI

Ludwig talking to birds

Ludwig loved his goldfinches in their cage, was excited by their plumage and its resemblance to his soldiers' military uniforms - the golden patterns on their tailcoats, and the special ones with secret white words scribbled there in cypher. *Stieglitz, Stieglitz,* he would address them - and they would speak back to him in their own tongue.

Distelfink, his uncle, called them. Thistle-finch. Perhaps this is how he would address or think of his rank-and-file troops - his little goldfinches.

Notes on optimum packing

Cartons each containing nine tins of enamel paint; an emptied carton, the inside of the bottom bearing the imprint/mark of the three by three rows of tins - an "oxo" grid full of Os.

In the Jewellery Quarter – in a Birmingham backstreet warehouse, cartons containing nine or even a dozen big square bottles of bright paint - the bottles square rather than round so the boxes could hold more and waste less space – an empty three by three or four by three grid waiting to be filled.

Secret nuclear research facility

In a shoe box?

Oh, Jane Burn

What an enigmatic alternate world your camera sidesteps us into - where trees are unnaturally green, and all those strange marks on the footpath... so many mysteries... why has traffic been diverted towards Ovingham? And what is that car vanishing into the distance? And what is the red car in the lay-by waiting for?

A wise woman

Schnee begs her beloved Amah to get the forbidden cards out once her mother has safely left the house. So out from their hiding place behind the mantelpiece comes the sooty-smelling old deck. Show me my prince again...

As her sight in this world grows dim, her sight in the other world becomes clearer. Here he comes... Ah, The Fool - a boy man who will never grow up and will never take any responsibility, will bring you much laughter but also much anger...

At a boot sale

Like a history of the world in 100 objects - the fort; old photos/postcards; rubber donkey; broken brass Napoleon; reddish-brown plasticine Margot Fonteyn; clockwork Woolworth's locomotive made of streaky semi-opaque orange plastic.

Someone has found a jar of farthings (Ben, if it's a reference to myopia).

Landscape with Figures

*A rich brown afternoon field curves down,
ridged as a ploughman's knee, to the track,
the corn as always too late to show;
ducks on the glassy pond seem ill-at-ease.*

*It's still and quiet. The light is harsh.
No birds sing in the dusty trees.
All trains here arrive or fail to arrive
at ten to three by the station clock.*

*The twin Miss Joneses, in pink and in black,
with nothing to do but meet each train
stand solidly glued to the platform and wait
for ever - or for no time at all.*

*The stationmaster seems only to live
to chat with the man by the churns and the truck.
Always unstable, the porter fell under
the last Up express. He's away being mended.*

Eric's search for order in the universe

(or at least in the world)

He likes lists, such as the list of the battles of the Napoleonic wars with notes of the nations whose armies were involved and the numbers of troops in the armies, with their date and outcome.

They help to bring at least an illusion of order to the chaotic virtual war games going on in his head, and the distracting needs of providing meals for himself and his invalid mother every day.

And his mastery of lists helped him become at an earlier period in his life, a mildly successful academic historian. Also a Doctor of Music, apparently. He understands history and appreciates writing.

Therapy

"Zoë," Harold asked his therapist, "do you mind if I call you Zozo? And may I put you in my book? Is it possible that in the early stages of your training, you might have been in the habit, after each of your more interesting clients leaves, of quickly jotting down a few of the things they have said to you?"

Martin/Ben might find in the big deserted house some of Zoë's jotted notes (in notebooks) and Zoë might become Martin's or Ben's (or anyone else's) therapist.

Ben's world was full of mysteries: how could a person born in May be an intellectual? How could an intellectual be a member of a men's hockey team? And how could a member of a men's hockey team have an intelligent opinion about the nature of smells? - such complexity!

Martin

Martin is a bit of a case. He would probably benefit from sitting down to talk to Zoë for a while, if that can be arranged. But we can understand his difficulties. His wife, lovely though she is, and practical and conscientious (as is he – conscientious, that is), does come from a long line of princesses and may well have absorbed some deep-seated attitudes that would prove unhelpful. Or indeed helpful but in a different way.

Martin says: As the hero of my dreams, I'm a fighter and a lover. I'm literally a knight in shining armour. I need to win. I'm frightened of boredom and of failing.

Stumbling home late one afternoon after finding himself at the edge of a copse on a hillside overlooking a wide empty valley, extremely hungry and with no signposts in sight, Martin has at length come across an isolated cottage that initially gave him hope that he could ask for directions and at least beg a drink of water and maybe a couple of biscuits to keep him going, but though he knocks on the doors, front and back, nobody appears. He looks in through the kitchen window and can just make out in the gathering dusk what looks like a body stretched out on the floor. He feels around in the earth under the window, finds a sizeable stone and is just raising it to try to break a pane of glass in the back door when he comes to, lying on his back on a pile of sacking in what appears to be a shed. The door is not locked and there is a water butt outside, where he slakes his thirst with a couple of cupped hands full of water. It is broad daylight. In the distance he can see a town built on a hill. He walks wearily on...

Welcome to Fallerton

Historic 14th century market town

Twinned with Bernstein, Austria

Not just twinned – modelled on, some might say, its church spire decidedly looking rather un-English in its onion-like shape. A pretty, tidy little town, with a few distinctly continental touches. This is the town where Mundy, Mundy and Vogel have their office, and the parking would be a nightmare. Martin was glad he was on foot rather than driving. He noticed the crows perched here and there about roofs and guttering like decorative accessories, looking for all the world as if they were waiting for something to happen on which they could comment. Had he seen Hitchcock's film The Birds? Does the idea of Hitchcock even exist for him, in his world?

Fallerton does actually have something of the air of a ghost town about its empty streets. Just out of town is a train station, of course, with an intriguing "mineral line" that runs to a small, dishevelled but still active mine, the Faller mine, that has been owned by the same local family for longer than anyone can remember. And what of the family? Is the town still surrounded by a forest? A plantation, perhaps? Or is there simply a vestigial stand of copper beeches left crowning a suspiciously round barrow-like hill?

Four millimetres to the foot

You know how blokes are nearly all interested in model trains – some blokes are more interested in the model landscapes that the models run through, and in how to make those miniature worlds as realistic as possible. Don't ask me why – I'm not a psychologist – though I would guess it has to do with control and with things being of a size that doesn't overwhelm one. There are shops scattered about the country that specialize in model railway accessories, and most of them have a section stuffed with racks of plastic bags containing everything from kits to build scale model buildings of every description, through packs of tiny telegraph poles, to bags of gravel, flock and grated plastic sponge dyed virtually any colour you could imagine, used to simulate grass, heather, rocky scree, pebbled beaches and the foliage of various types of trees... But, unless you're a millionaire, when you are working on a large layout, you tend to make your own coloured gravel and foliage, and you do something called scratch building to produce your own houses. This is what Olivia does.

The world that is growing in her attic includes something called a mineral line – remarkably reminiscent of the site at Bernstein where Schnee's descendants at the turn of the 20th century were digging out amber for export. But Liv's pride and joy is something called a Faller road system. I could cut a long story short here, but I don't know why I should…

Ben's questions

At the age of nine, Ben Harper was not allowed by his upbringing to know the answer to many questions. In fact he was not allowed to know many questions. At the age of eleven he was maybe getting an inkling of some more questions to which he didn't know the answer.

The boy assumed the writing on the tin of jam was Dutch, but didn't pursue the train of thought to wonder why apricots should come from Holland. Sufficient source of wonder for him was in the packaging. At home, jam came in ordinary-sized jam-jars, and they would have various kinds – strawberry one month, maybe raspberry the next and then perhaps bramble jelly for a change - but he could see that it was sensible, if apricot was the sort of jam Uncle Felix liked best, to get it in a big tin. The same went for the marmalade for breakfast. A new vision of the possibility of a simpler way of living, and thinking about living, came to Ben's mind. You like to paint, so you paint. You like a particular kind of food, so you get it. Why on earth did life at home have to be so complicated and hedged about with ifs and buts, when it could be this simple? Ben cut himself another slice of Uncle Felix's home-made fruit cake.

Ben liked to ask Uncle Felix his serious questions, for the same reason that he would ask his Dad rather than his mother his serious questions when he was at home. Often with his mother he used to feel that she was fobbing him off rather than taking his questions seriously. He supposed it was understandable because obviously she didn't always know the answer but didn't like to admit she didn't know (unlike his Dad who would sometimes admit he didn't know something but more often tell him to "look it up in the dictionary". In fact he was told this with such frequency that halfway through asking a question he would interrupt himself and say, "I know – look it up in the dictionary" for himself). At least his Dad tried: his mother sometimes seemed to think his questions were not important enough to bother to try to answer.

Anyway, one day he asked Uncle Felix whether our prayers come true. And, if so, what happens when two people pray for things that clash? Like, for instance, if I pray for it to rain and someone else in the same place prays for it to be sunny? Uncle Felix said what would happen in that case would be that the other person would have the experience of it being a sunny day and you would experience a rainy day. A pretty annoying typical grown-up answer in some ways – the kind of thing you might expect to be told by the vicar (who told Ben at confirmation classes that the sign of the cross stood for "I" crossed out) – but the more Ben thought about prayers happening and how you experienced different sorts of days, the more sense his uncle's words seemed to make. Good old Uncle Felix.

Eric at Sheerness

At Sheerness (or was it Shoeburyness? Sharpness? the place anyway where Derek Jarman had lived among the radioactive stones and the barren sand and cultivated his imagination and his bleak little garden of spindly weeds*) along the path to the shingle and the sea pinks, the wind rattled the chain link fence alongside the pale tarmac. Eric recalled seeing a big maroon Humber Super Snipe saloon stuck firmly between the pale blue upright posts of a rusty gateway the driver must have thought was plenty wide enough. There were scrapes of rust and powder blue paint on either flank of the high broad bodywork, and no-one in sight. Obviously the driver had gone off in search of help rather than try to wrench free his pride and joy all by himself and risk doing it even more damage. The sight put Eric in mind of Seymour Glass's bananafish.

His wonderful Henrietta had said he could come back and collect her at ten to twelve, and they would go and find some lunch…

(*it was Dungeness)

The scruffy area by the brook by the scruffy sheds

... made of old corrugated iron - that might be the same location where young Ludwig and his chum made the detonation.

Harold en route to Venice

To get to Venice on a coach trip, you have to spend more than a couple of what feel endless days being driven across flat brown miles of France where all you can see through the windows is earth and the occasional distant, tiny spire of a village on the horizon. I was lucky in that I had my wife as a travelling companion, and that she does not feel the need to be always talking. I think she probably had a book or magazine to read. And I had my notebook – it was at a time in my life when I was usually working on trying to write a poem or two. But for many of the passengers (we were seated in about the middle of the coach, and the racket came from the seats at the back, behind us), it seemed that to keep their sanity, they must TALK. And talk they did – a relentless yammering that was impossible to ignore or blank out of one's consciousness.

By the end of the third day of this, I was pretty uptight and ready to scream, and by the time we were beginning to see rocks with snow on them as we drove up into the foothills of the Alps, I was developing in my mind and in my notebook the alter ego of the lady assassin Sula who would be able and willing to commit with her lightweight Glock the required quadruple murder to relieve my tension.

Martin lost in the Triangle

Oops! Here I go again, finding myself somewhere and not being able to remember how I got here. Must be old age. Still, it doesn't seem to have any repercussions for anyone else or affect them in any way.

Pretty sure we drove down this street five minutes ago - I remember that silent face at the window under the streetlight, like the ghostly person at the top floor window in Cezanne's painting of the maisonettes at Jas de Bouffan.

VII

The fortress town of Pignerol in Piedmont

At some point during the campaign against the Dutch, the Sun King and his minister of war were in the mirrored gallery poring over the long rows of tables with the detailed relief models that gave an aerial view of his kingdom and possible battlefields.

From "Optimal Packing and Depletion" (A. R. Davis)

"Shortly thereafter, Fernandez de la Vega and Lueker (1981) showed that, from a theoretical point of view, one could do much better than this. For any e> 0, there is a linear time algorithm A, that has an asymptotic worst-case ratio no greater than 1+e. More precisely, the guarantee provided is that A,(L) Q (1 + c)OPT(L) + 0 (c-*1. Unfortunately the running times for these A, are exponential in l/c. This drawback was eliminated, at a price, by Karmarkar and Karp (19821, who found modified versions of the A, with running times growing only polynomially with l/e. The "price" was that programming complexity was increased by several orders of magnitude. (The modified algorithms use the ellipsoid method of Khachiyan (1979) and Griitschel et al. (1981) as a subroutine, as well as subroutines for finding near-I optimal solutions to the NP-hard "knapsack problem."

The fort in question

May no longer exist, human beings being, as they are, sometimes unable to recognize other people's treasure when it actually resembles old-fashioned crap. It used to reside in the back or bottom of a wardrobe in the "master bedroom" of a pre-war semi in the Yardley suburb of Birmingham. Initially it would present as a flattish plywood box large enough, I suppose to hold a very large cake, with paper pasted on the sides to give the appearance of a brick footing overgrown with ferny vegetation. This I believe, would be meant to represent the inner wall of a moat. In this sense it represented to a boy of about four years of age a small red-brick castle. In view of the item's venerable age it was to be treated with great respect. It had probably belonged to the small boy's grandfather and was only to be played with carefully and calmly. Inside the box or base were various wooden elements, again covered with printed paper of 'red brick' effect, such as corner pillars, walls, and sections of round arch that could be assembled – with what seemed to the boy considerable concentration, trial and error and the exercise of remembering – and all held in position by short metal pins that located into corresponding holes – into the semblance of a Victorian military barracks with a central courtyard or parade area.

Associated with the fort was a certain quantity of lead toy soldiers, mostly or all, I believe being Cameron Highlanders of approximately 1910 vintage in smart kilts with a tartan of dark green crisscrossed with lines of white and red that must have been the devil to paint.

This of course, as I see now, makes them almost certainly items that would have been given not to Ben's grandfather but his father, who was born at the turn of the century. Curiouser and curiouser – Ben's father never seemed to treat the toys with a proprietorial air – more a custodial one, as if they never belonged to him but were being held by him in trust. A little bit of a mystery.

We wondered: did our Cameron Highlanders hunt, catch and roast woodlice in a jacket of clay as gipsies roast hedgehogs? And did they taste like scampi? Lobster?

My Dad had got from somewhere big glass bottles of paint, red, blue, yellow, black and white, that we spent ages turning upside down and shaking to disperse the bands of darker thicker paint from the bottom until we could see that all the colour was mixed and even. I remember the label – "Canning." I don't know if he had only just "acquired" them (he liked to be what he would call "mysterious" about where things came from – which the younger of my two sisters thought was romantic, but it made my mother, who of course knew him well, and even me, at the age of only four, suspect concealed something maybe a little less than honest. A shame, because he was, in general, a very Good and "moral" man. Just maybe weak - a trait he passed on to me, I fear. Though what I think I mean by 'weak' is in serious need of frank examination). That was probably my very first lesson in colour theory, as Dad showed me how to mix a little blue enamel paint into a small pool of yellow in a tin lid to make a green (not the other way round, he said, or else the blue would overwhelm the yellow and you would never get to green). Then just a spot of black to darken it. That went on to the soldiers' kilts one by one, and they were laid out in a row out of further harm's way, to dry while we put out tin lids red and white for the square lines we were to add.

My Dad got out a book of tartan designs to show us exactly how it should be – the original soldiers' paint had become so battered by being played with and knocked about in combat that it was hard to make out the pattern – I couldn't believe how many different variations of Cameron tartan there were, and we eventually decided to do the one that was a compromise between looking really pretty and colourful and being too complicated to try to copy on a kilt the size of a little finger fingernail. We had to mix some white and red paint together to lighten the red and make it opaque. It would have disappeared if it had been put on neat, it was so intense. Doing the thin lines with a very fine brush he called a pencil was great fun. Once we had added the widely spaced network of red lines we put on exactly midway between the white, it made a lovely pattern. I think my sister and I worked out a kind of production line way of working, with her putting on the white lines and me adding the red ones. We were all for trying to curve the lines to follow the curve of the hip where a soldier was kneeling, for instance, but Dad insisted we just continue to make the squares square – he showed us some illustrations from a Tintin comic where someone was in a coat with a large check pattern – the check pattern was drawn with the verticals parallel to the sides of the page, and the horizontals to the top edge, regardless of the position of the person's body. It was weird, but it did look right on the page. Something to do with what he called Ben Day tints, which we didn't really understand at the time. And trying to do it the way that we wanted to would have been impossible and would have driven my sister and me barmy. Mind you, I'm not at all sure he was right about doing it that way on a three-dimensional surface like a Highlander's backside, and I think we would probably have just said, "Yes, Daddy," and carried on doing it the way it looked right to us. He had probably lost interest by then anyway (he liked to get people started on a project, explain all he could about the best way to do it and then leave them to get on with it for themselves). And to be honest, the figures were so small that the exact disposition of fine lines on their little kilts was such a detail that nobody was really likely to be going to notice or criticize. And it was really satisfying to see how smart they all looked once we had finished. The green was a bit too bluey in places on some of them, I thought, but that was just me being a perfectionist and critical of my sister's work. The actual tartan did, I think, have black square in the centre of each square of red lines, that we were not even going to try to reproduce.

It was good. And I must have really found it exciting, as the memory of doing it has stayed with me for sixty-five years.

Eric going to the Kinema

Dr Eric Downey was also shortsighted. Late one afternoon at the end of term, when his history class had covered the syllabus and had taken their exams, he decided to share with them something of the lessons about relationships he had learned in his youth - how, when his fiancée wanted to see a particular film, he had paid for her ticket but decided to sit and wait for her in the cinema foyer since his extreme short-sightedness meant he could not enjoy the film. Afterwards, the boys shook their heads in disbelief - for them a visit to the cinema with a girl was not about enjoying or not enjoying the film.

The narrator

Harold sat at a space he had managed to clear on the corner of his old cluttered computer desk in the box room he thought of as his Ivory Tower (though it was actually emulsioned Housing Association Magnolia like most of the other walls in the place) scribbling away as usual by the light of the single low-energy overhead bulb in the cheap tin light shade, ignoring Mrs Thing chuntering away downstairs trying to get him to go down and help fold the ironing the girls had brought back the day before. He had murdered her several times.

Oh, shit, the computer's started going slow and pausing for seconds at a time before what I type appears on the screen, thought Harold, exasperated, just when I'm getting into a bit of a flow. Is that a hint from somewhere that I should not be wasting writing time on Rex's mother and what might or might not be going through Olivia's mind? When I should be giving some thought to actually progressing the plot in some way. Plot? What plot? No, look, this is not the kind of book that has a plot like that – it's not a murder mystery. There's not a crime to solve, or a dilemma for the hero to get out of. It's just about a bunch of people and their ideas and my ideas about stuff that comes up. Sure, I may never pull it off and make it into anything that anyone will want to read, but I've gone too far now to start trying to make a "story" out of it. If you want incident, go find yourself a nice Tom Clancy. End of rant, and the computer now seems to have got over its tantrum, so I can get on with what Olivia was doing. All right – thinking.

Where was I…? No, it's no good – I've lost my flow. Make tea.

The kettle had boiled (he'd heard the click as it switched off in the kitchen as he was typing), so he went into the kitchen and made tea. Got out the milk jug and sniffed it as he usually did, to check it had not gone off. It smelled all right, but to be on the safe side he poured a drop into his empty mug and tasted it. Ugh! It had gone off, had that bitter edge. He tipped it in the sink and got out a clean jug and put fresh milk in it. Now do I have a dilemma of my own here? Do I actually get up and get on with taking the tea tray upstairs (leaving you, dear reader, sitting waiting), or do I keep typing about how Harold got up and took the tea tray up to his wife – which will leave her lying there like lady muck wondering where I've got to with the tea she asked for a good half hour ago? And I need to have a shower anyway. Ha! Go!

Ludwig's memorandum

How many troops shall we need in order to be certain of victory and a good show on parade? But I wish to be seen by posterity to have been an enlightened commander: No more rape and pillage - my soldiers must be instructed to ask politely, "Voulez-vous promener avec moi?"

It's almost

As if the key to the whole thing lies somehow in the pots of morning glories along the edge of the veranda.

An old chap lives the other side of the close. Outside his front door is a bench he and his wife would occasionally appear sitting on to enjoy the afternoon sun in the summer. Now, in January, there are big flowerpots on it - one with a tiny Christmas tree he recently planted, and a couple of others with stumpy rose bushes that are beginning to bear bright healthy looking leaves. Every couple of days, I notice that the pots have been rearranged on the seat, though I have not seen him move them. Perhaps he quickly does it early in the morning and evening, so that the rose bushes will catch the best of the sunlight during the day but will be slightly protected from the frosts at night.

In the real world, flowerpots range from the size of a coffee cup to something a person (a thief in Ali Baba, for instance) could hide in - which I would call ginormous. On the Layout, a pot the size of a thimble you might get from a Christmas cracker would be absolutely ginormous... and of course, at 4mm to a foot a coffee-cup sized pot would be virtually invisible...

Max again

Maybe at the party: maybe not, what follows can be said...

Hi, I'm Max. I have always been here. So I can describe everything that happens or has ever happened. Including, possibly, Harold's thoughts. Certainly everything he writes. Can I lie? Can I mislead you, reader, or hide things from you? I'm also, I think, Felix, somehow...

Extract from a letter (?) from Max

Rule 1: what you truly believe will happen will happen. This is not the same as saying that what you truly believe is so. MM&V reconcile conflicting beliefs under Rule 1, which is why, in some ways the world is such a very odd place. If it should be absolutely impossible (if ever – figures are not available) to reconcile two conflicting beliefs, then each will be made true for the person who believes it. This is part of the explanation for what is called madness.

Hi. On the other hand I'm Harold Thing. I can say anything I want, as it's me writing this book. But who writes the things that happen "outside" the story? Is that Max? Nothing can, by definition, happen outside the bounds of the book.

Who is creating me?

I'm simply Ben. I can tell you what I did and thought at various ages, and what I have been told. But I can't tell you for sure what is going on in other people's heads – though I can imagine or make an educated guess – or what happens in the next room. Only in this one.

Aka cosmic ordering

So I went through the green door and down the short paternoster to the Universal Emporium for some rolls of big paper and a couple of boxes of sheep. You can never have too many sheep – one box goes nowhere at all.

Sparrows

As he sat at a military desk in a military hut among a few dozen similarly just-barbered young military recruits and half-listened to an uptight staff sergeant droning on about the difference between a fifteen-inch step and a thirty-inch step and precisely how to salute when wearing a headpiece with a visor or a headpiece with no visor (which he could read for himself in the pages of the drill manual that was on each desk in the room anyway), his eyes and then his mind was drawn to the sparrows on the bird-feeder that he could see hanging on the bushes in the Colonel's Lady's garden just across the corner of the parade ground outside the window.

Ben at Uncle Felix's

Here it's like heaven. Listen to those silver birches. If I were a Red Indian I'd be able to build a canoe. Nigel is stupid. He doesn't know anything. Just because his Dad's a painter and decorator, he thinks he knows the best way to paint a board - well, my Uncle Felix is an artist and when he tells me to make the brushstrokes in every direction it's the best way to do it. If I'd done them all straight, it wouldn't have been like a canvas to paint on. Stupid Nigel. Rich boys, boys with rich Dads, have no idea. Just because they have big bikes and Hornby Dublo train sets and everything, they think they know it all.

It's great here, like being in the Malayan jungle or Japan in the war, with all that bamboo. And all those pine trees belong to my Uncle, and the sheds – the really broken down overgrown ones you can't really get into for nettles. And that one with all the bundles of old brushes hanging up. I wonder why he kept the old brushes and didn't throw them away. I mean, I know my Dad would have kept them, but then, he's a bit more 'practical' than Uncle Felix, and he'd have warmed them over the gas stove to soften the glue and tried to pull the bristles a bit more out of the ferrule, wouldn't he, to be able to use them again. I like the word ferrule. I like learning the right words for things – specially when it's words that stupid rich kids don't know.

I'm going to climb that pine tree again tomorrow and see if my secret rations are still there on that branch. I love dates. Like I love prunes. And I love Uncle Felix's special tea – even though it's not sweet. I was going to say I wish my Mum would mix her own tea – those smoky-smelling black woody tea leaves and the lemony Earl Grey – but I don't even think that: home tea is different, comfortable (even if it's kind of sweet and tasteless) – not special and grown-up and foreign. I love that my uncle has lived in China, where there are pirates and you have to put chicken wire all over the top of the boats to keep them off – even if that was in the nineteen twenties when he was a young man working out there. And I love that he lived in America, in Los Angeles – even if he does say the name wrong. Everyone knows it's Los Anjellies, but he calls it Los Angheles with a hard g. Though he ought to know, if he lived there. Maybe that's the way they used to pronounce it in the roaring twenties.

It's great when we sit out on this veranda like this to have tea, when the wind blows softly through the trees and bamboos. When we are by the Chinese stone statues that look a bit like Uncle Felix, I wonder why he looks a bit Chinese (I don't think he can be at all Chinese really, but maybe it kind of rubs off on you if you live there a long time). It's those wrinkles at the side of his eyes. I love his face. When my Dad was making that bas-relief of him in plasticine, it was in profile, and he made his head too nearly spherical to look like him. But then, Uncle Felix gave up on trying to paint that portrait of me he started, didn't he? So I can't complain.

I love the way he shuffles his feet when he walks about the bungalow in his slippers like a big old shambly bear. My sister brought me back a carved wooden bear with a pincushion glued on its back when she went on a school trip to Switzerland, to Berne. Bears are the patron animals of Berne, and I think Bern must mean bear in German, which they speak there when they are not speaking French. I happen to know (because I looked it up in the dictionary like I'm always being told to) that Bernstein is the German word for amber – so I suppose that means they thought it was a bear-stone.

Perhaps because bears have a lot to do with pine trees and it's pine trees that make the resin that turns into amber when it gets fossilized. And I love Uncle Felix's corduroy trousers. The knees are like ploughed fields on two hills. I like to wear old clothes. I wonder what it feels like to be a bit famous – even if it was his brother Rupert who was more really famous and made that bronze torso on the black wooden block and had books written about him. Funny to have a sculpture your brother made and have to treat it as if it's a special work of art. It's a pity Rupert died. Though I like Uncle Felix best. Maybe that's why he seems sad sometimes. That and his wife dying.

He writes me letters and sometimes he sends a postal order and he signs the letters "Your Affectionate Uncle" every time. It's good of him to remember my birthday. I never remember anyone's birthday – not even my sisters'. I call him Uncle even though he's really Mummy's uncle, so he's my great-uncle. One day he started telling me about when he was in the trenches (he was in a highland regiment - it must have been the First World War) and the machine gun bullets whizzed past "like wasps." That might have been when I seemed to be afraid of the wasps who came after the jam. I imagine in his calm way he would have shown me that wasps won't harm you if you don't interfere or get in their way. Or he might, of course, have just efficiently pressed them down in the jam with the back of a spoon and drowned them. I think he would have thought it was wrong to drown the wasps, even if they do have stings. Either way, my eight year old self would have been mightily impressed. At that age, I had not really been anywhere. I used to wonder if they had some kind of wasp radio, because if you hurt or killed one wasp, more wasps would come straight away, like Messerschmitts when a Spitfire gets one.

It's great to live in a wooden house, and not bother with housekeeping except when his sister's coming. Gaby. That's Gabrielle. Then he spends a whole day running the noisy old vacuum cleaner, beating the dust out of the rugs and hanging them out of the windows and sweeping the house ready for her, and I get to sleep on the day bed in the big room. I like that. The day bed has a black-painted curly frame, like something out of an Egyptian pyramid or the Regency, and it's not really a bed. It's covered in woven raffia like the seat of a bentwood chair, with the weaving in that lovely pattern that's not quite honeycomb but eight-sided instead of six-sided shapes all over. When I sleep in the big room I can look at all the Reader's Digests in the bookcase – he's got hundreds of them. I liked to read the Towards More Picturesque Speech parts – it's American. Americans must have a thing about speaking more picturesquely. Usually I can tell which is the right word. And I like That's Life – it's kind of little jokes. I don't understand some of them. I did read a whole long condensed book in one Reader's Digest called Twenty-Four Hours Under The Pistol of a Killer. And years later I found it again in a French edition – Vingt-Quatre Heures sous le Pistolet d'un Tireur. I'd learned French by then.

Of course, the best thing about being here is Uncle Felix's studio where he does his painting, and when he lets me stand behind and watch him painting – he has paint in great fat tubes because he uses so much, not the ordinary little tubes you see in the art shops. He has a pair of pliers he keeps there just to unscrew the tops off the tubes. I loved to watch when he squeezed out the yellow paint to paint an evening primrose. It was thick and buttery, and he mixed it with white paint. White Lead, it's called. There's Titanium White, too. I can't remember what he said the difference was. You always mix the colours with white – Mummy told me that, I think. It makes the paint go further, but it also does something else I don't remember. He mixes the paint with a palette knife, not with a brush – though sometimes he does put some of one colour into a blob of another with a brush. And there's something called Megilp, that you use to stop the paint drying too quickly – or to make it dry more quickly. I don't remember which, and to make a glaze. That means it's transparent. Megrim is a nice word, too – it means migraine, which I think is French, and I suppose in the 18th century, when we were worried about revolution and afraid Napoleon (they called him Boney) might invade England, people didn't want to pronounce it the proper, French, way – even if they knew what that was - so they Englished it into Megrim. To be patriotic.

When he wants me to go down to the village to take the accumulator from the wireless to the man in the bike shed who recharges it, he gets the money out of the wide drawer in his Studio. It's a big wide shallow drawer and it's got all this money scattered in it – coins and notes just lying there. I'm quite ashamed that I have once or twice taken money from there when I was desperate to get a gun or some soldiers or some other toy from the shop in the village after my Postal Order from Mum was all gone. I don't know if he knows I took money, but I felt quite ashamed because he was so old and trusting. He doesn't seem to count it or to pay it any attention at all. Not like at home where they are always worrying about having enough money. My Dad earns seven pounds a week. I know, because I asked him once and that's what he said. Usually we can't afford things. And if it's going to be your birthday you can only have something that costs half a crown. That's two and sixpence. Once when we seemed to be "a bit better off" my Mum said I could have something that was five shillings, and we went up to a big toyshop in Birmingham to choose. I looked in the window, and there was a seed drill with a brown cart-horse that I thought I might like. I think that was five shillings. It had a plastic harness, brown.

At Uncle Felix's, I climbed back up the tree to look at my supplies of dates but there was an earwig inside the cellophane packet and it fell out and I didn't like it. I know those pincers on an earwig don't sting you, but it feels as though they might. And I think they might give you a nasty pinch.

There are lots of tools in one of the old sheds. I cut out a panel of bark from the branch I sit on in the small pine tree where the earwig was. I love the smell that comes out of the bark when you cut it. And there's lovely thick, clear sap under there, like the tree's blood. It's called resin. It sets in the air when it dries. If it was a maple tree it would be sweet, but it's not. I've put a label of paper in the square place I cut out, saying my name (my Red Indian name Little Owl from the I-Spy books) so anyone who climbs up that far will know it's where I was. When I come here again next summer, it will have clear sap dried over it like glass, and you'll be able to read it through the glass like a notice to say I was here.

With a little axe from one of the sheds I cut a slot in the bark further down the tree, like they do to get rubber in a rubber plantation, so the sap would run out, but I don't know what you can do with pine tree sap. It doesn't make rubber. If you get some on your hand it goes sticky and brown and you can't wash it off. Though next time you look, it's gone.

In the front part by the gravel drive that goes from the two Blue Cedars on either side of the white gate all the way to the Sun Room at the corner of the house, there are apple trees and big green cooking apples fall onto the ground. I get the job of peeling and cutting some for stewed apples to go with our breakfast. I like cutting the apples up into wedges and taking out the pips and the parts with grubs in and the little bits of hard skin from the middle and peeling away the green skin. I sit at the table on the veranda to do it. At tea time we have fruit cake that my uncle makes. He had a wife called Lily but she died, so he's called a widower and he lives by himself, but he seems very calm and contented. He used to love her a great deal, Mum says. He used to be a scoutmaster to the boys in the village, and they're very polite to him when they go past. They call him Messer Plermtree.

Anyway, he whistles for the birds and they come for cake crumbs at the table. For breakfast we can have Puffed Wheat, which is all right, even if it doesn't taste of anything, but it's nice with stewed apple. We have brown sugar – the hard sort, not soft brown like we sometimes have at home. And sometimes there's a junket. If there's too much milk and some has started to 'turn' we pour it into a big shallow dish and add something called rennet and put it on the pantry shelf all night. Next day it's junket – white and a bit thick and smooth and it tastes a bit sour but it's lovely with brown sugar or with Puffed Wheat and stewed apple. At lunch or dinner time we have mackerel which is my favourite – lovely firm fish we buy in the village or from the fish van – or Uncle makes curry – and the fish has a terrific pattern on its skin, sort of dark grey and silver, a bit like the pattern on the dragonfly I saw by the pond. Sometimes Uncle Felix spoons some yellowy curry powder onto his rice with a big silver spoon and stirs it in.

There's a round fish pond in the back garden. Most of the garden is just like a jungle – with tall birch trees high up all around whose leaves are always moving, and in front of them are lots of pine trees with bark that is a pinky colour, especially in the evening. In front of them are a lot of bamboos standing about in tall golden clumps, hiding the scattered sheds all overgrown and mossy and licheny and broken-roofed. And long grass everywhere, not mowed like the grass at home. The only part where the grass is shortish is the part just nearest to the house where there are the flowers that Uncle Felix picks to make paintings of – lupins especially and some roses, I think. And this pond. No, he doesn't make paintings of the pond.

He paints vases of flowers – my mother was particularly proud when one of his paintings was used on the front cover of Woman's Own magazine, but that's the way my family are: they go on as if commercial success for your art was the worst kind of sell-out, but then they all swank about and crow like fury if they or someone they love actually makes a sale. Of course, if someone outside the charmed circle of family and close friends makes a success of things, that's also the cue for cattiness and imagining the worst possible motives or really poor taste on the part of the buyer. It's all to do with the odd mental gymnastics required to justify being poor while believing that we are really superior beings with impossibly refined taste. That and the female side of the family being a bit Cancer-heavy, with my mother and the girls having July birthdays and most of the other relatives I knew about being close enough to that date to have a lot of their planets also in Cancer. Probably.

Otto's broomstick submarine

Otto, in his youth, had spent a lot of time designing and making a broomstick submarine - reminiscent of the time I spent making my solid balsa model of a Hawker Hunter aircraft, which had entailed what seemed like hours of painstaking carving and sandpapering to achieve the correct smoothly curved shape, followed by repetitive filling, sanding and filling and sanding again to give a suitable faultless surface to paint. Otto was more practical and less of a perfectionist, though he did make considerable efforts to mix the correct shade of greyish green enamel paint with which to paint his submarine. He actually soldered cut-out brass vanes to a spindle in order to create a mechanism that he believed would allow the craft to move up and down in the water like a real U-Boat.

VIII

There is always a moment of choice

Eric is talking to Hen. As usual, he is mulling over the moment when he "fell" for her. She accepts that they are in love with one another, but she doesn't 100 percent believe in the fated quality of their relationship. She tells him that there is always a moment at which a person could either allow themself to step over the line into being in love or refuse it and choose to turn away. Sometimes difficult, but always possible, she says. His eyes go distant as he tries to remember that moment and believe, but he is too wrapped up in his feelings of euphoria.

Max on the other hand, a wiser man, had felt the tug of love for Olivia, but resisted it, feeling the temptation to surrender but then choosing instead to continue with what he saw as a more durable, more workable kind of relationship with the potential for a broader spectrum of satisfactions. A romantic commitment seemed a dangerous prospect that could have been disastrous for the wellbeing of each of them.

Harold at Tesco

You know how it is, Harold thought to himself. Even with your wife in the car, you're driving past a lay-by in a leafy bit of wood and there's a woman with the sunlight catching her big head of deep reddish dyed hair, leaning against her car for a smoke or to talk on her mobile, and immediately you're away with her driving into Scotland or somewhere, in a movie dream adventure. Like the way there are days when it's as if they've let everyone out of their homes – everywhere you look there's something wrong with the way people look. They've got oddly-arranged features or an expression that suggest they are not quite all there. I know you shouldn't be like that but it happens. Like in the autumn there'll be a day you go into Tesco and almost every woman you see there is beautiful and stylish as if they were a glamorous spy or something, and you wonder why they've taken so much trouble with their appearance when they were just going shopping. It can't be to attract a man – slightly mature women anyway have probably had as much to do with men in their life as they want. It must be to do with self-expression or self-respect – and I suppose I ought to reciprocate by thinking of them with respect rather than as sexual objects. Which I do, in a way. I mean, I'm not looking for a liaison, or I don't think I am. I just enjoy looking at them, as it were, aesthetically. The more I say about this the worse it sounds, and I know I shouldn't be like that, what with being a married man. Though I guess if that's the most immoral thing I do in my life, I'm not getting on too badly.

For a moment I had a thought that made me feel very happy, like dreaming that there is no such thing as chocolate and waking brokenhearted, but then remembering that I'm in the real world where chocolate does exist – but like a dream, I forgot it and couldn't bring it back.

Harold had read somewhere recently on the internet a woman writer quoting someone very unlikely (could it have been Nietzsche?) saying something very perceptive about poetry. Although he could not remember at all what it was that was said, he was totally confident that at some point his brain would prove to have squirrelled the quotation away safely in the appropriate place and would produce it during some early morning contemplation, to contribute to a useful thought.

Let's try to understand Max

How would it be if Max, having built up during the seventies, eighties and nineties a massively successful architectural practice, became bored with making money, had a bit of a breakdown (when he realised his son was forming an attachment to Olivia, the modelmaker he himself was in love with), "threw it all up," dismissing his partner architects and assistants, leaving Olivia in control of the country mansion that had housed the firm and, looking for a more satisfying project - a retirement village, disappeared to start again, looking for a bigger project in Paris or possibly Dubai?

That then would lead into the scene where Max is sitting at the coffee table in his living room drinking in the middle of the night, and to his conversation with Olivia or Rex or both.

He wakes with a jerk, from a long, complicated dream involving libraries and research projects about the sources of science-fiction film and television, and finds that his mind has become clearer. It must have been the alcohol that was causing him to have muddled and worrying thoughts. Distracting. He turns off the light and sits quietly, letting his eyes adjust to the darkness. The room is not completely dark: there are little red lights on the phone on the side table, on the television in the corner of the room and on the power lead connection under his desk, as well as a pale glow coming from the closed laptop at the side of his desk chair, as well as a light vertical streak at the edge of the window blind, where the street light comes in a little. In fact, as he sits he begins to be able to make out the shape of the various pieces of furniture and the framed items – plans and photographs – on the walls. So I can really see in the dark, he smiles to himself. Big deal.

It is strange to realise afresh every now and then, at moments of contemplation like this, that he is, actually, capable of everything and anything. The word omnipotent is so casually bandied about in the literature and in theological discussions that everyone, even me, he thinks, seldom stops to realise what it really means.

Good party earlier. Nice to actually meet such an assortment of people.

On the kitchen wall is a cheap-looking tin spice rack enamelled in black, with a brightly coloured promotional picture for a comic book – prominently red, blue and yellow. Is that what the lizard was looking for? As a safe place to sleep? Or as somewhere to hide and spy on the people who spend time here? Nearly five o'clock now. Go back to bed.

The Innovative Cheese Products Company

Olivia worried about there being an ageing demographic in the Triangle and introduced the cheese factory to provide employment opportunities and slow the migration of young people to the cities.

For a while the area might be known in the local rag as the Cheese Triangle.

Sir Nigel Gresley

The Sir Nigel Gresley was originally to be called Bittern, in line with the more famous Mallard, but was renamed in honour of its designer Herbert Nigel Gresley CBE, who died in 1941. It was the 100th Gresley Pacific locomotive, with a top speed of some 113 mph.

One can almost imagine these pipe-smoking engineers sitting at a table sometime in the 1930s and arriving at a committee decision that their hundred-ton creations should be named after various species of British waterfowl.

Ben and the pond

Ben had read somewhere about being able to make a working motor boat out of card or paper, powered by a drop of oil – just exactly the kind of back-pages-of-a-weekly-children's-comic rubbish that would have appealed to him (gullible nine year old fool) – and to about a million other small boys. I know – let's blame it on Nigel. So Nigel had put Ben up to the idea, even brought along the actual issue of the comic to show him (Nigel probably had sussed by now that Ben didn't really like him, but he needed to add him to his meagre stock of "friends" – probably having alienated most of his other peers with his stuck-up ways, and probably too much of a snob (or his Mom, more likely. I don't think his Dad the decorator would have had much in the way of airs and graces or social aspiration – though who can tell?). And there it was: instructions. It showed you the shape to cut out of your piece of paper – a simple boat shape, with a keyhole-shaped cut-out "channel" leading from the central circular "reservoir" via a narrow slit or slot to the rear edge. 'Put the boat gently on the water' (he did) 'and add a single drop of oil' (he did) 'to the reservoir.' He did and, lo and behold, the boat gradually and steadily moved ahead across the pond, spilling out a thin slick of oil across the surface behind it as it went. It slowed down, and he added a further drop (he'd found the can of Three-In-One in one of the abandoned sheds). Mmm, this was fun.

The following afternoon, when Ben returned to the house at tea time after a couple of hours fighting the enemy among the bamboo thickets, he was completely unprepared for the angry figure waiting for him by the pond. "It's too late now, but tomorrow, my boy, you are going to help me clean out this pond and hope you have not completely destroyed all the creatures that were living in it." Looking down for the first time, the boy saw that there were indeed a number of dead fish floating on the now grey and, he noticed, extremely smelly water that was streaked with slimy rainbows. It turned out that in his ignorance and stupidity he had laid a film of oil all over the surface and thereby effectively suffocated not only the fish but also probably a large population of frogs, newts and all kind of other insects and larvae that had been living out their blameless lives for years unseen in the water and in the mud at the bottom. So next day the two of them, old man and great-nephew, knelt on the edge of the pond together in the morning sun after a virtually silent breakfast, and used sheet after sheet of old newspaper to soak up the oil, and then filled the pond up to the brim with fresh water, the boy praying that somehow they had done it in time to rescue from a horrible death at least a small percentage of what had been living in the bottom.

Hen's Halloween party

There was punch – in fact there were two bowls of punch, each labelled on a piece of folded card: "Social Lubricant" in front of the left-hand bowl, "The Real Thing" with an inky spiky drawing of a bat, on the other. The punch table was theoretically being supervised by Rex, with the intermittent assistance of a couple of girls, but he didn't seem to be taking the responsibility completely seriously, and all three tended to wander away and leave the two bowls unattended. At such times, various of the very much younger guests tried their luck by surreptitiously sampling the mixture with the bat label and then wandering away to a corner to see how it might be affecting them in terms of blurred vision or inability to walk upright without support. Most seemed disappointed by the outcome of their investigations and then felt obliged to pour scorn sotto voce on the concept of grown-up-ness in general.

Schnee, now in her eighties, had created a bit of a stir and localised hilarity by getting confused by the labels and taking away to her place on the sofa a generous glass of the stronger one.

At the party were:

Jean, looking distracted and actually worrying about having left Daphne at home with Susan to babysit.

Olivia, trying to have a serious talk with Rex.

Rex, who is a pretty Hamlet-like character if the truth be known, and tends to try to distract himself from what he knows he should and at some point, obviously will, be doing, by flirting, yes, with girls (and even boys? – maybe).

Eric Downey – invited by Hen as one of her strays/lost souls/people in need of her salvation.

George Harper senior – maybe – if I/Ben can handle the confrontation/being in the same room.

Ben of course.

Zozo. Remind me who Zozo is: she's Zoë Salt, the newest of the 3 doll cousins, the right-hand one, nearest the bedroom door (do you want a family tree? I'll do one in a little while – promise! Your favourite, remember? Upright, hopeful, almost or probably with a ponytail. Yes, but whose daughter is she? Can't, I think, be Rex's – we shall see – so probably in some way Ben's – though her Dad's car, before the Bugatti became Rex's transport, belonged to Louis. So Zoë is Louis' daughter. The one he brings home books for. And would that be the same Louis who develops into a megalo-obsessive Wagnerite? Hmm? Would it?

Owen, for some reason getting slowly drunk in the depths of his potential for being or having been Otto of the terrible ankle. And he is besotted with a girl who turned up once somewhere in a white duffel jacket.

Not at the party for various reasons were:

Susan (Jean or Martin's mother) - why not? (if Martin is staying at home at the cabbage garden cottage, babysitting).

Otto as himself.

Martin – babysitting and doing some other thing he doesn't want Jean to know about. Namely…?

Family tree as promised: Zoë and Henrietta are cousins – though the family secret may be that Zoë is actually adopted. Henrietta and

Margot (think they) are sisters. Ludwig married Schneegwyn. Schneegwyn's daughter is Susan. Susan's daughter is Jean. Zoë is unlikely to be Jean's sister. We don't know who Hen and Margot's parents are… so far. Perhaps Pru and George.

Could Hen and Margot be Ben's sisters? Or is Zozo his sister? That's more likely.

Love, as they say, had found him late

Eric Downey's youth had passed in quite single-minded academic endeavour. Young Henrietta said she was not the gold-digger some people might think, taking up with a much older and quite well-off man past his prime and not physically prepossessing - in fact, in most people's eyes, a bit of a bore. But she did love him, and their relationship was mutually beneficial and satisfying.

Harold's intention

Harold: I didn't intend for Eric and Olivia to meet. I thought they would inhabit different worlds. Given what she is, though, I suppose it was inevitable.

And, by the way, if Ben and Ludwig were ever to meet in the same room, they would quite possibly both disappear in a puff of white smoke and cease to exist.

Olivia is largely Lydia Davis, with a touch of Siri Hustvedt and a trace of the time-traveller's wife.

Renaissance Studies

I am surprised more people don't murder their partners - so many women and men are so manipulative or overbearing or both.

The machinations of local village politics were positively Byzantine.

Olivia's husband Andy had been a lecturer in Renaissance Studies. So he knew a thing or two about the meaning of Byzantine, she thought absentmindedly, as she lay half asleep in bed one Saturday morning at the beginning of a cool July. And probably the right way to pronounce it and Renaissance.

He also probably knew what the Levant was. Wasn't there a word - Levantine?

Vaguely thinking back over what he had just written, Harold thought it was not clear or precise enough: he should have said it was Olivia's ex-husband she was thinking of, and made it clear that he was still a lecturer, though not still her husband.

Behind the Colosseum: how Olivia becomes the girl in the photomural in the Costa Coffee shop

Rex is sent to Rome to set up an Italian branch office and invites Olivia to join him there.

While she is there, Olivia goes into a souvenir shop and can't resist buying a kit to build a cardboard scale model of the Colosseum, with a vague intention of introducing it to an empty area on the outskirts of Springton on the layout, and so sometime later she can be seen standing in the tall narrow street behind the partly-ruined building [which the locals refer to as The Arena], looking up at the pale sky above the aerials, washing lines and telephone wires. It looks like rain. She is feeling uncharacteristically powerless and a little anxious - which shows in her eyebrows and the line of her lips. She is anxious because Rex does not seem to have heard her call, and she begins to look around at the edge of the cobbles for some small chips of stone that she might be able to throw up against the window or the shutters to attract his attention. She cuts a forlorn figure in her long, floaty white skirt, strappy sandals and skimpy vest, hugging herself against the chilly breeze.

This morning Rex was still feeling tired after spending a couple of hours or more last evening in the restaurant arguing with two shop owners about the ethics of making a profit from tourists who did not understand the currency, so when they found that they had not enough bread for breakfast, Olivia had offered to walk to the shop, leaving Rex to catch a little more sleep. As the street door slammed behind her, she realised that she had not picked up the keys to let herself back in and was trying to attract his attention to tell him to throw the keys down to her.

Felix in wonderland

Felix in Wonderland would be the title of the book I would write – if only I had time. My, what a life I've had, looking back over the years. And here I am now, living out what remains by myself in this wooden house that Lily loved so much. Sorry, my dear, that I can't keep the garden as you would have liked it. But I do my best, and I'm looking out for Prudence as I promised you, and now her boy.

I have discouraged his ambition to follow in his father's footsteps and enter into the uncertainties of a career as an artist. But the young idiot has poisoned my fishpond and destroyed one of my trees, albeit unintentionally, and I strongly suspect he has taken money from me.

Margot's vocabulary

Disparate, thinks Margot, and says it. We three are disparate.

We are indeed, says Zoë.

Desperate, says Hen. You may be - personally I'm hopeful. Positive.

I know what you mean, Zoë tells Margot.

Discrete, maybe, says Margot. Are we discrete, then?

Well, I hope I'm discreet, says Hen. I need to be, and my Eric.

Your Eric? says Margot.

Your Eric, says Zoë, needs to be discreet -

Not discreet - discrete, says Margot. Spelled differently. Like in concrete.

You and your dictionary, says Henrietta.

I suppose we're a bit like broken concrete, says Margot. Hardcore.

I'm sure I don't know what you mean, says Henrietta.

"Strange, strange, strange," she says to herself. "How strange, strange things are!"

Trouble with words.

Cousins, thinks Margot, looking in her dictionary. Confusing.

Not sisters, but like sisters' daughters. Only I'm an orphan, too. And adopted. Very confusing.

Don't worry about it, says Zoë. We might all be orphans, adopted.

Zoëtrope: Zoo - zero zebras.

OMG is there going to be a murder, or a body, at the hotel? Or maybe a disappearance? YES! She was so excited she wanted to jump up and down, but she was holding her suitcase in one hand and her overnight bag in the other, so she just gave a little jiggle as she walked across the reception lobby with its marble chequerboard tiled floor.

Clocks

It's ten to two in almost every "scene". In some that means early morning (late at night). In some it means late lunchtime, but in some, it can feel like ten past ten. Like Ben, Eric is shortsighted and, even with his glasses on, may well misread the tiny hands on the tiny station clock.

Notes to self

Electric cookers are so slow.

To heat the saucepan of Big Soup, the line on the knob needs to point SSE: if it points SSW you will be waiting forever for it to heat up, but if you make it SE, the soup will boil and go runny.

Re Chinaman's sleeves: it felt as if he became an accelerator or whatever the word is for that enormous underground circular tunnel at CERN. Tucking his linked hands into the sleeves of his dressing gown seemed to complete some kind of electrical circuit in his body and concentrate his chi - if that doesn't sound too new-agey and Glastonburyish.

NB Chinaman's sleeves are also like a straitjacket. He hugs himself.

Does amber float?

Yes, in salt water, but not in fresh. A useful test. Salt sees clearly.

IX

An extraordinary century

The hundred or so years from the late 17th century to the late 18th century seems extremely important in terms of inventiveness: late enough to have lost the crudeness and religious/political extremes of the Civil War period but a little earlier than the time of enormous Napoleonic wars and the stultifying Victorian atmosphere.

Perhaps Prince Ludwig's ridiculous negotiation with his military tailor can take place within this century that does not quite match up with the calendar century. Harold thinks of the period as "Queen Anne" - which may or may not be wildly inaccurate.

Is Martin a spy?

I sometimes wonder if Martin is actually a spy. It would explain a lot of strange things about him. He does seem to have a secret life of his own, but it's as if it's a life he's not in control of. So often he is unable or says he is unable to explain where he's been. And he sometimes disappears for quite long periods of time. But then he will suddenly arrive somewhere with no explanation. For example – the day I told him Mother and I were going to take Daphne for a picnic on the hills, and he was supposed to be at work. We got to our picnic place, and who was there leaning against a tree at the edge of the field but Martin. No real explanation was offered or anything.

"Meet me at the Bar Napoleon, and bring the money"

The Bar Napoleon, of course, was in the Hotel Méditerranée, near the seafront. You might object that that is not a likely name for a hotel in a town like Seaglass, but this is clearly not quite the real world and not the real Somerset.

Blue Bugatti

When he is on the Continong, Rex becomes more flamboyant and drives a powder-blue Bugatti garaged in Rome. He enjoys Mussolini's long straight roads as well as the dusty country ones with the geese.

Amber

"...the treasures with which I expected every search into those neglected mines to reward my labour, and the triumph with which I should display my acquisitions to mankind"

(Dr Samuel Johnson, from the preface to his dictionary)

Of Kings Ness: "Anyone bothering to walk for hours with head bent, staring at the beach, could find here million-year-old amber from Northern European forests" (Tommy Wieringa, from 'Caesarion')

Jean: A gene for youthfulness?

There was this spooky-looking bloke I noticed, kind of trying not to stare at me but obviously interested in something about me. For a minute, I was afraid he maybe had his eye on Daphne but, no, I checked and it was clearly me he was focused on. Maybe I reminded him of someone else. There is some actress I've seen on television – can't remember where, maybe even in an advert – who I remarked to my Martin was quite like me about the eyes. And of course, folks are always wondering about my age, apparently, because I have the air of being much younger than I am. Or so they keep saying. It's – well, not embarrassing, exactly – but funny. Only I do get a bit tired of having to tell people how old I am. It's as if they don't really believe me even if I show them my driving licence.

Harold saying the unsaid

Sort out the things you (and the reader) might need and want to know. List the mysteries, and the questions – then ask the only reliable witnesses (Max, of course, and almost certainly Olivia) the questions and write down what they say in reply. You could even ask them to explain. The only possibly reliable other witness is Harold – but do we want to involve him? (why not?) and can he really be trusted? Does he even necessarily know the answer/s?

Incidentally, which of the other characters do we think are honest or truthful or capable of telling the truth? And which are not, and why?

I kind of think the only characters I would not trust to tell the truth (if they knew the truth, and to say if they didn't know) would be Margot and Harold – of course – he's a storyteller. George and Pru would possibly try to evade the question if they felt the answer might embarrass or displease you. But, for what it's worth, they would feel guilty about doing so. Ben might also lie, as would Owen. I think Eric thinks he's honest and truthful. But under pressure he could well fib with the worst of them. Otto would only lie about politics or military secrets or maybe to win a battle. Or to a Frenchman. Do I have too low an opinion of human nature? Felix was elsewhere for much of the time, so would not express an opinion.

Eerst Graad

Eerst Graad, it said on the tin, with a picture of apricots. It was extraordinary to the boy to have jam on the table in a big tin that you had to open with a tin-opener in the form of a bull's head with stubby conical horns. It was also a revelation to find that he could understand whatever language the label on the tin was written in. At school he had started learning with the rest of Form 3A something engrossing called "phonetics" with their new and fascinatingly different form master Mr Pritchard who wore a black beret. This was in preparation for starting the study of French the following year.

Mr Pritchard had the boys chanting the funny alphabet that was in the new textbooks he had handed out and they had to discover these new sounds that they were not even aware existed and then practice them. Weird guy, the boys concluded, but then Mr Pritchard proceeded to win them over by teaching them, would you believe, in the form meeting that followed assembly every morning, to make tiny flying model aircraft with a matchstick in which two slits were cut to hold the paper wing in the correct curve to actually provide aerodynamic lift. In no time, the entire class were flying their tiny planes about the classroom. Another time he showed them how to take cuttings from (was it a fuchsia or a geranium?) some plant or other and – unbelievably for a bunch of normally scornful and rebellious kids (yes, even at the tender age of – what? – thirteen?) they all became briefly, dedicated window ledge gardeners.

He also, I recall, when it turned out to be a severe winter, taught us how to make ice cream – create very sweet custard by stirring jam into it and set it outside on a frozen pond overnight, I remember. The main thing was that he treated us as if we were intelligent and interested adults, and so, of course, that is what we became. He also ran the Model Aero club where it was that I spent ages sealing, sanding and sealing again (or vice versa) a solid balsa Hawker Hunter model. God knows why – at home I was building, then or at a later date, a flying Fairy Gannet, and had also managed to make a large flying glider model with a Jetex engine. Lots of scope for smells, smoke and parental-avuncular interference. I also remember a boy (forget his name) who actually bought from me at least one tiny model plane (a biplane of my own design – "all made out of my own head" as they say, "and wood enough left for another") that I made from left-over scraps of balsa wood. Extraordinary – Harpers didn't sell things they made, not for actual money. Certainly not with such a sort of casual ease. It comes back to me now, out of the blue mists of the past: the boy's name was Beresford.

From an end of term report:

Benjamin tends to proceed by applying a formula (which, to his credit, he may have arrived at through clever analysis and thought combined with trial-and-error) rather than by the preferred route of applying his undoubted intellect, talent and imagination.

Zoë

Zozo loves her "unreliable" Dad and gets on well with her sisters/cousins. Sparky and sparkly and eager, she has a GSOH and will go far in whatever field she settles on. She may be also Jean. Or even Ben's sister.

Zoë, I ask her as she sits in the upright upholstered chair opposite my seat. Who are you, what are you, what do you do, and what are you looking for?

Hiya, says Zoë. Woo – a lot of questions! Not sure I know the answer to most of those. I'm looking for fun and for something useful to do. What I do is get people to talk to me about what they want and don't want. What I am is a therapist in supervision, but what I really am is a confused person. I suppose my hope is that by helping other people to discover themselves I might learn to find me. I'm ninety nine percent sure that my Dad was a gentleman called Ludwig. Mum said he was Ludwig Swanson, and he came from a very wealthy and old Hungarian family. Jean's my middle name and my surname is Salt. I believe I have a brother called Benjamin, and I don't know if Henrietta is my sister or not. Henrietta is lovely. Aptly we call her Hen, and she is a mother hen. She doesn't look anything like a hen – she looks like an old-fashioned film star – but she is always taking people under her wing and looking after them and trying to rescue them. Like Eric for instance. She kind of thinks Max Mundy might be her father, which would make Rex her brother. Are you following any of this? Feel free to make notes. Or I can lend you a recording machine. But I'm afraid I'm not a trustworthy witness. I'm still trying to find out all these facts myself.

Downey's jokes

Misunderstanding on the car ferry tannoy: Drivers are requested not to start wearing jeans until instructed to do so.

As I said to my friend, the Holy Roman Emperor, (Large) noses run in my family

Reply: ALL the noses run in my family. Boom! Boom!

The invisible man was standing there, wearing just my slippers, trying to see himself, toe-to-toe in the floor-to-ceiling bedroom mirror. He stood there as if holding an invisible gun. I saw through him straight away.

He said he would like to become an unclear physicist.

And he insisted on referring to an ambulance as an ecnalubma (he was that kind of autistic smartarse.)

Prologue

I am determined to get this book written. I have called into existence these intersecting cross-section slices of the universe, where Olivia is forever swooping about in her enormous loft to build her own version of the remembered model landscapes of the Sun King that she saw in a basement in France all those years ago; where Ben is forever ferreting about in the earth and on the beach, remembering guns and an Uncle; where Ludwig is doting on his beloved Maman, her goldfinches and his pretty soldiers; Eric is trying not to be pathetic in the eyes of his beloved Henrietta or anyone else; Martin is struggling with issues of ambition and comfort and family love and security; crazy Otto is mourning his youthful whiskers; and the dolls mean to party like it's 1954 and there's no tomorrow. These people have somehow taken on an independent existence. They persist, and their lives impinge on each other. And somewhere, the endless war has not ended. My job is to write them - into fuller life.

I don't know from where, but I find I have this unshakeable faith that somewhere among these nondescript snippets of phrases and ideas and images will be found an amazing story and a book, just as somewhere up there among the monotonous and seemingly endless vistas of pine trunks and rocky slopes could be found an entry into a world of virtually priceless and beautiful treasure – and just as, of course, among the inchoate and confusing mass of all our night after night remembered or disregarded dreams, can be found the key to reveal that incomparable jewel – our real self.

The big donkey

Some railway modellers, especially those with large layouts, will use OO scale for most of the layout, and then for buildings in the furthest part of the scene, switch to the slightly smaller HO scale, to increase the illusion of perspective. Olivia experiments with this idea, so that the cardboard chateau near the back of the board is probably modelled at HO, as are the buildings in the depths of the forest – and also, of course, Schnee's miners, while their big donkey (whatever his name is) will be an OO figure among HO figures.

Harold: The Alabaster incident

Aged about 13 (so it would have been 1955) I had a monumental crush on a fifth- or sixth-form girl called Juliet Alabaster. She would have been 16 or 17, and was one of the school's sporting champions. She and her friend Claudette Wilkins would have netball or hockey practice after school finished at ten to four, and me and my friend Alan Baker would wait to trail adoringly along on the other side of the road as the two girls walked their bikes together the length of Reddings Lane before they got on them and went their separate ways home - leaving us two gormless kids to make our own forlorn ways home too. A strange sight we must have presented, all in our green school uniform blazers – the girls with the green and gold braid of school prefects, and us boys not yet of that rank. The two girls were aware of our shadowing them but chose to ignore us completely, except on one notable afternoon when I trustingly stooped down to talk to a dog at the front garden gate of a house we passed, and was bitten on the nose for my trouble. Juliet teasingly called across the street to ask if I would like her to come and kiss it better. This was so far outside the "rules" of the situation, and yet at one level precisely what I craved, that I was speechless and presumably made no coherent reply. We were worms, far beneath the notice of these two teenage goddesses whom we were only permitted to worship from afar for their fair ponytails and exciting eyebrows.

Looking at the A to Z Birmingham map now, in 2017, I see what a constrained existence it was in those years - our whole life happening around the districts of Tyseley, Acocks Green, Hall Green and South Yardley: bounded by Warwick Road, Olton Boulevard and the Coventry Road.

Some of us moved out, on and upward, presumably, to follow careers in the wider world of academia or a variety of professions; some of us remained rooted in very local soil and local thinking. Yet here I am now, sixty years on, elsewhere in the world but still or again kind of rooted in my thinking. Aspiring to a wider frame and fame but bounded and bonded by immediate concerns and commitments.

The two cousins on the platform

Martin is leaning on a luggage barrow outside the waiting room. The station is deserted, except for someone on the opposite platform and these two young women who from the back could almost be twins – both exactly the same height, though the thin one in black has a little pill-box hat that doesn't suit her and makes her look older. The other, to whose arm she is clinging, is bareheaded with plentiful curly dark blonde hair. She is wearing a pink suit. Either she is the plumper of the two, he thinks, or she is sensibly wearing more layers against the chilly wind that whips through the station from time to time as if a door had been left open somewhere.

Some of the figures on the platform are conscious of playing a part - the expectant girlfriend, the businessman who is going to be late for a meeting, and the bunch of yokels hoping to catch a glimpse of the returning war hero.

Harold's book

Making his way home after paying in a dozen cheques at the bank, he caught a glimpse of a different world he might inhabit – a world where life is simple, straightforward and logical, not fenced about with moral decisions to make about every action or idea – so much clearer than the murky overgrown forest he felt he would be re-entering when he reached home.

His book was not going well – in fact he often wondered whether it was worth continuing with it. At this rate, he thought, he was never going to get it finished. Whichever section he sat down to work on, it would feel as though another section was most in need of attention, so there were whole hours when he sat at his desk and wrote nothing – or only despairing scribbled notes to himself that he then crumpled into a ball and tossed towards the waste paper basket. If getting the promotion depended on turning in a completed book, he might as well give up. On both – and let Mary think him a failure.

I've never really understood Owen. I mean, he's a good looking boy – curly reddish hair, mischievous grin, especially when he wants to charm you if you're a woman, and those somehow quite round brown eyes that look directly at you and that he knows can be quite disarming. I know he used to sometimes say something outlandish or deliberately provocative and then give me that level, unblinking, slightly enquiring look and wait a second for me to respond – that's if he could resist bursting into laughter. He was always laughing at things people said – especially himself. I think he got it from his parents, who were both, in my recollection, what I would call jolly people, his mother in particular. When I first went round to their steamy little prefab I was surprised at how young she seemed – as if she was of a different generation from my own parents, whom I was conscious of thinking of as Victorian – not that I think I had a very clear idea of what I meant by that. I must have been only about eleven years old, I suppose. His Dad could be quite moody - had been a coal miner, I believe, and I do remember him losing his temper with Owen over something he said. They struck me, too, as quite an intense family, all of them.

About the Bismarck thing, I don't know if he's serious, or trying to have us on with a straight face.

But, anyway, all that is irrelevant to where we are in the story at the moment.

I wanted to say something about being able to hold in one's head at the same time two (or more) mutually exclusive beliefs, such as a belief in astrology or reincarnation, an omnipotent God or the impossibility of a loving God in a world of cruelty, or multiple universes or quantum physics…but also about the strength that comes from only believing one thing at a time as Bismarck presumably did, or Napoleon, or Eric prior to his reconstruction at the hands of Henrietta.

Now behave, please, machine. I need you to work properly. I'm going to type like the wind for twenty minutes and see what comes out. The story so far: Somebody – Otto in the guise of Owen is on his way to the Bernstein Castle Hotel to meet Schnee, who happens to be wearing a white duffel coat – something Owen finds sexy and probably irresistible.

Young Otto and Ben as Ludwig have caused the explosion in the garden behind the palace.

Ben is on his way to, and has also arrived and is spending time at, Felix's.

Rex has invited Olivia to Rome.

Max is in a bit of despair, but has enjoyed the party.

This is all a bit circular, which is fine, by the way.

Jean has fed her baby, Daphne.

Prudence is getting to accept – possibly – the idea that Ben needs to do what he's doing, but she is also wondering how to cope – boys are so alien to all she has ever experienced. At least George is home safe from the war in France where he served as an engine fitter in the RAF.

The boys came here on their bikes

On their way to the Scilly Isles for two weeks of camping, Ben and Nigel spotted the big old house across the fields and decided to investigate, with a view to putting up their tent in the grounds for the night. They hauled their bikes across the railway line, scrambled up the embankment and found a gap in the iron railings to squeeze through, alongside an abandoned broken sign, *The Bullfinch Retreat for Perplexed Gentlefolk*, half-hidden among the bushes. Naturally, always open for mischief, they crept through the overgrown rhododendrons and tried the back door and, surprised to find that it opened, went in to explore. Most of the dark and dusty rooms were empty, though in one up the stairs they found the remains of a model railway platform with a few little figures – a group of passengers and a porter with a luggage barrow, still firmly glued in place.

Back in the garden was a pile of split black plastic rubbish bags as if someone had bagged up ready for disposal the accumulated paperwork of several generations of families and individuals who had inhabited the house, but then had abandoned the project and rats, cats, passing curious foxes or children or just the wind and the rain had got into the bags and scattered the jumbled fragmentary archive to the four corners of the grounds..

There were great wads and bundles of assorted letters and notes of conversations, broken business account books, old invoices whose blank backs had been used to write bits of family history, and the notebooks... dozens of notebooks and journals and diaries dating back for years, some with pages torn out. Many of the assorted notebooks were virtually illegible – as if written in twilight with no intention of rereading but only "getting something down on paper" – but a few were different: obviously written at various different periods in somebody's life and carefully. Dating from times when it seemed important changes were going on in someone's inner or outer world.

Ben started to read an exercise book filled with someone's scribbled night thoughts from a previous century.

Whatonages

*The bloke I was following
just kept on walking.*

*It was ten to ten when he left
the station, and he kept on going.*

*My feet were getting sore – not sure
if my shoes were wearing thin
on these hard pavements
or if maybe they were too small.*

*I could not fathom where he was headed
and I had long since forgotten
what I was following him for.
Was he a spy, or indeed was I a spy?
Or worse – government agent? Assassin?*

*We'd left the houses behind now,
passed the gasworks and seemed
to be heading out into the open country.*

*A few shops ahead - we passed them,
all closed. It was by now after all
Sunday afternoon, or felt like it.*

*He didn't seem to be carrying anything.
Why had they sent me? He must know*

*I was tailing him, but he didn't turn.
Neither did he slow down. I began*

*to feel quite light-headed. The sun
was lost in white clouds and no wind
disturbed the quiet. Just the sound
of our footsteps. No cars.*

*The road ahead turned
beyond an isolated house
with a high hedge. I hurried
to not lose sight of my quarry,*

*but when I reached the bend
the road was empty. Just trees.*

X

Olivia on the bus

For some reason she had caught the bus to get to work this morning – had woken rather later than she liked to. She sat on the upper deck, partly because she felt a need to think, and sitting on the upper deck was somehow conducive to taking a broader view of things – if only she could keep her mind from straying into its favourite game of guessing who people were that she saw on the streets below and wondering where they were going and why.

    She caught sight fleetingly of five or six figures struggling in an alley behind a tall railing with a gate in it. Looks like two men or two men and a girl in the process of being arrested. Maybe they got found out taking advantage of another man who trusted them. And let them live in his house without enquiring too closely how much the one man was charging the girl/how much if anything the girl and the man were contributing towards the costs of the place - nursing vipers in his bosom. Maybe questions had finally been asked that didn't have to be answered for the truth to come out. Let's hope nobody is going to have to look over his shoulder and be careful from now on.

    She wanted to think about something Rex's mother, Mary had said about how we each create our own reality. That was the sort of thing Mary said all the time. Now Olivia found Rex's mother in many ways an annoying woman, whom she suspected of being very shallow and of batting about ideas or even just words she had heard or read and had only partly understood. It didn't help that she was foreign. Olivia kept thinking of her as Armenian, which she knew was wrong, but she always had to make a real conscious effort to remember the right word – some kind of Freudian slip, she imagined. One day she would sit down quietly and give it some serious thought, work out what it was about the word that made her mind uncomfortable and unable to easily bring it to consciousness. Heavens, she thought, as she put her purse away, don't I sound the serious one!

A man she thought she recognized distracted her from her thoughts for a moment as she watched him step up to the kerb across the road and pause to let the traffic pass. He had clearly missed the bus. Her thoughts returned to Rex's mother and her half-baked ideas. We all create our own reality. When she said it, Rex's mother probably intended it to mean that we can affect what happens to us by our attitude – that's assuming she actually gave any thought to what it meant, rather than just trotting it out because it sounded vaguely comforting.

The cream-painted double-decker bus with the navy blue stripe has now become part of the layout. Hooray.

Life is so weird it's hard to believe we are not each of us making it up, she thinks as she catches occasional glimpses of another world and way of life: a white refrigerated transit van bearing the legend "Temperature controlled distribution - daily runs to Manchester and Leeds" so some driver's life is sketched out there in all its relentless routine in a single line.

NB it's entirely okay for the various accounts of people (and events and places) not to exactly tally or agree.

Mrs Downey's inside

The little blokes in the Day-Glo jackets pause in their labours, lean on their shovels, tip back their white hard hats, light a fag and wonder how they are ever going to clear this blockage.

"Don't worry, lads," says the foreman, "just give it time. So long as nothing else comes down the big pipe, it'll gradually get cleared. It just needs time. Nothing much more we can do for a couple of hours - might as well go back to the hut and put our feet up. Take a break."

England from the air

To fly over much of England, even today in 2021 in a small plane, is to be struck by how green a land it still is despite all the people. Yes, you see towns and roads, but the overall picture below is of mile upon mile of fields and hedges, trees and scrubby woodland, everywhere green. With just the occasional isolated building or cluster of buildings. In the early nineteen-forties, from an RAF Spitfire or Hurricane, it must have been even more widely green below. It would have looked, in fact, not unlike the landscape part of a model railway layout. Or a much smaller version of the great Middle European Forest.

A couple of things may be going on here:

Either the Multiverse Model - we may each of us be dreaming, imagining or otherwise creating our own model of the universe, and may each inhabit our own bubble as a facet of a sort of consensual whole - or the kind of vaguely Darwinian Accident model - there is no creator, no purpose, merely a string of accidents driven by the forces of nature, or (this being the age of the uncertainty principle and quantum physics) both may be the true picture and there may be no absolute ultimate reality.

There's a sense in which we each create the world we live in.

Ben on myopia

There came a point, when he was in his mid-teens, when he began to realize that he had once or twice failed to recognize a friend across the street. He sometimes was unsure whether a bus approaching him waiting at a bus stop was the one he wanted or not. It reached a kind of critical point when he suffered the embarrassment of putting out his arm and having a bus stop for him before seeing from the number on the front that it was not the one he wanted. On the first occasion that this happened (bear in mind that he was a somewhat dreamy young man and his mind was often elsewhere) I believe he boarded the bus anyway – not wanting to make a fuss or seem an idiot – obviously got off at some point and made his way back, presumably making up some story for his family or teacher if they asked where he'd been or why he was so late getting home or whatever. But anyway, the problem didn't go away. Grew worse, in fact, so eventually he had to have glasses.

- Bang! Revelation – he could see distant detail with his glasses on almost as well as when using his telescope: each tile on the roofs in the next street. Suddenly friends on the other side of the road and approaching buses were no problem. Life went on with that particular difficulty solved. Real life doesn't bother with a plot... but arguably the major result of that visual breakthrough for the boy's psychological development was the realization that short-sightedness in the purely physical sense that had been affecting him was linked to short-sightedness in the sense of a personality trait. With glasses, he would probably never be quite the same person again.

Zozo's Dad

Louis was impossible – lovely but impossible. He haunted bookshops and used to bring home books for her. One such was a storybook that went "Ludwig and his Mama lived alone in a pretty little house." Well, it wasn't a little house, it was a small palace. And they didn't really live there alone. They had a small army of servants to look after them.

Zoë's Dad had once had a bit of a Road To Damascus moment. She found a note addressed to her in one of the books he gave her: "there is more to life than fame, position, soldiers and money." That was why her real first name (which she hardly ever used these days, and hardly even remembered having been given, was Eppie, short for Epiphania (would you believe Epiphania Salt?)

But it was many years ago, and the reason why she had once been so intrigued by the story of little Epaminondas.

Class war comes to the Layout

"What do you call the place you keep your car," he asked her on their walk – "is it the garij or the garahge?"

Eric (Doctor Downey) would be appalled at Harold's cavalier treatment of the facts of history - apropos of which, the class war/civil war is still going on - though Ben felt he belonged to probably the last generation that had been brought up to speak 'properly' and say garahge rather than garij.

Olivia on art as autobiography

The more detail I create in my model, the greater the detail I become aware of in myself.

A little character smaller than the joint of my thumb, placed alone just so on an empty road that leads off past the closed warehouses towards the distant foothills, becomes a habitation from which I can look out with eyes weary of loneliness, tired of solitude yet still curious and eager to see what they will discover beyond the next turn in the footpath and the nearer trees.

Schneegwyn at the hotel

It was the afternoon of a mild early autumn day.

"Come on, Schnee," the 'girls' called back to her as they got up from the terrace tea table overlooking the bay and headed up the slope towards the hotel, "It'll be getting chilly out here soon."

Schneegwyn's white-spotted navy blouse hung loosely from her thin shoulders and she struggled into the boxy jacket of her thickish suit as she got up and followed the others back into the warmer lounge. "Come along, Princess," they said kindly, holding the door open for their elderly friend. Schneegwyn's eyesight was beginning to grow dim, though her eyes were still bright. She wore fairly thick-lensed glasses. Her bones seemed to have shrunk somewhat, and her once-luxuriant golden hair had become sparse.

Hotel they are calling it. Hotel my eye, as Lord Nelson would have said! More like a cross between a hospital and a prison camp, it was, and here it was we pitched up. In a lovely spot, no disputing that – view out over the bay from the front rooms – and a rather nice terrace there that caught the sun from morning till evening, so the old ladies were happy. Oh, yes, there were a bunch of old ladies who would gather out there once they had come down from their rooms when they'd woken from their after-lunch nap and lingered over tea and cakes.

And the staff looked after us well, even the wounded soldiers.

And let me tell you, some of the wounds were unbelievable.

Schnee learns to move into the present and give up or adapt the values of the past. She also has to deal with losing her sons/servants as a means of vicariously achieving what she herself didn't/couldn't. She represents both the strengths of the past and its weaknesses.

"Let me recognise myself for what I am," she addresses her face in the mirror, "someone passing through the world, time and life like a tourist." She thought, whatever may happen to me now, even if it is ghastly, at least I have known what it is to be in love and to be loved

The detonation of the bullet

I remember there was violet light falling that day. Owen and I seemed the only ones awake. We crept through the palace like thieves when we had taken the tin box of pin-fire cartridges from the wardrobe in Father's [the General's?] dressing room. Outside by the kitchen garden wall, the dogs were dozing in the late summer sun beneath the ripening peaches and there was hardly any breeze to disturb the flies resting on the magnificent banks of manure that were ripening behind the ranks of glasshouses. The older middens looked dry and hard, with grass growing on them. I told Owen to find a firm place to poke the bullets in, while I searched along the gravel path for some suitable pebbles like David preparing to meet Goliath. We'd decided we could take three of the cartridges and space the others out in the tin so that no-one would notice any were missing.

After I had seen where he had put the bullets into the soil, we stepped back towards the wall and turned to look at our targets, but couldn't see them clearly from that distance. I'd thought the bright brass circles of the cartridge bases would show clearly against the dull grey of the dry manure, but Owen had buried them with a stone resting against the firing pin of each, in a row about a foot apart. So we replaced them with white stones to be visible from where we would be standing, a few yards away.

We took it in turns to take aim and throw our pebbles at the white stones, and we kept missing and ran out of pebbles so I had to find some more, Owen keeping a lookout in case one of the gardeners should appear. We carried on, neither of us wanting to admit what terrible shots we were or to move much closer to our targets like girls. I think we were both almost ready to give up when it happened – I scored two more misses and then there was a furious bang and muck and soil and gravel exploded in a ball in the air and showered down on us amid a cloud of blue smoke and that lovely smell of fireworks filled the air.

White smoke. I just typed "a cloud of blue smoke", but it wasn't blue. It was white. White smoke. I can smell it now. After a second of deafened stunned silence the dogs began to bark and we heard an ominous clear sound of panes of glass falling out of the side of the nearest greenhouse. We ran off without a word, through the gate, and hid in the edge of the woods until the dogs stopped barking and the smoke had cleared.

It took us quite a while to find the two un-detonated cartridges. A dark snuff-coloured hole big enough to hide in had appeared in the side of the giant compost heap and was quietly steaming in the sun, and we eventually picked up the smashed empty bullet-casing from the foot of the wall. God only knows where the bullet went to. We had thought it would bury itself deep in the dung-heap. Maybe it did.

Paint and smoke

"Start a new Paint and Smoke file," said the muse to Harold in the night.

Is it the 1920s when Louis, Zoë's unreliable Dad, brings home week after week, payday after payday (from the secondhand stalls in the city) all kinds of often totally unsuitable (ask his wife) books for Zozo - or is it maybe the 2020s? (and please note in passing how nearly ZOZO = 2020 – what can that possibly mean or portend or be about, Hmm? Answer me that if you can, if you're so berloody clever). And I'm talking here about *Zoë in Wonderland*, *Stahlschlüssel*, *Paint and Smoke*, *The Artist and the Built Environment*, *Prescient Millicent*, *Optimum Packing and Depletion*, and other standout or goto books of that ilk that feature on Zoë's bookshelves. That last title, by the way, links rather to another of poor Ben's lifelong obsessions – the one where he almost continually muses, at some level, on the idea that the more you cut or grind something (yeast, boiled potatoes, chalk) into smaller and smaller pieces, the more of that something you can pack into a given space. Which seems self-evidently true for certain things, but Ben's Scorpionic Pluto-ruled side, with its aptitude to carry any train of thought or behaviour to extremes, worries about how finely you can, in fact, chop radishes or grind walnuts or limestone, and whether there comes a point at which the substance vanishes, or to all intents and purposes vanishes. And the implications of that possibility.

There are times

There are times when the entire universe seems to be conspiring to make me feel suicidal: conversely there are times when the universe seems to be conspiring to make me happy.

The ducks seem ill at ease

And no birds sing. There's a waiting silence because an explosion has just happened in the garden of the big derelict house whose railings separate it from the railway line. Expecting clouds of blue smoke, one is surprised to see instead white cotton-wool drifting through the trees.

Eric's head

I have in my head now this list of things I have to do that I can do. This is unusual. What happened to all the things I didn't know how to do? The only one I can remember was solved by simply waiting until the other person involved in doing it got back home, read my email and said they would do it. Moral: be patient, and let other people do their part. Travel a bit more lightly.

Otto/Ludwig/Eric: growing up, I had aunts and cousins and a tutor/regent. Then I had a couple of college chums...now I only have spiders and the birds to talk to.

"had a friend once in a room

had a good time but it ended much too soon"

A whole dynasty of sparrows

The snippets of tunes (songs?) running in someone's head – "we run 'em in" etc

Harold: Like a séance

There are these mediums whose faces will take on the features of the "loved one" who has "passed over", as people say, who are in that line of work. The dolls' faces, seen across the room when I haven't put my glasses on, are like that too. I half imagine expressions there.

As with the personages on the Tarot cards - and from the world at large - I read into their faces the emotions and compunctions that I project back to myself, so that the rooks perched in a row on the ridge tiles, for example, will be croaking to one another under their breath "adulterer!" or whatever the case may be.

XI

Max on divinity

High time I came to terms with this entire omnipotence thing. What does it mean? And does it matter? Olivia would give me that "What are you like?" look and try to explain her point of view to me – how we have this enormous responsibility to our people, a duty to manage our resources efficiently and think about the planet and the future and so on. Rex, I know, would say no, it doesn't matter in the slightest, it'll all work out all right in the end. Trust the process – all that New Age-y twaddle. Sorry, son, I don't mean twaddle. It's just that the pure hippie approach doesn't work. We know that now. I know the boy isn't a hippie…but he does have that tendency to bunk off work whenever the spirit moves him. Ha! That's a good one – which reminds me: I really must get someone to find out what exactly is the situation with him and Olivia, what's going on there.

Difficult to know how to handle the cult of personality. That's one of my big questions. How can I separate the role, the uniform, call it what you like – the what I am – from the person, the preferences, the who I am? I know (well, I certainly feel) there are others up here /out there somewhere. But I seem to be the one who's been entrusted with the power. Which is nice of course, in fact mighty fine - wouldn't change it for the world, all that – but…I sometimes wonder if there isn't a supreme Supreme Being who has decided which of us should be the main one, the Main Man, the Main Event. Maybe it's done on a rota basis - that would make sense and account for all kinds of odd things about history. We do seem to have wandered in and out of fashion over the millennia. Or do I mean centuries? Whatever. As Olivia might say.

Maybe it was time to make another visit to the attic of Nigel's house and see how the figures in the landscape were shaping up. He reached for his homburg.

Harold: Don't forget Fairest's shop

The photo albums, the shoe boxes, the sideboards - and the bundles of letters, scrapbooks...and the mail order emporium where Jean works, sourcing and sending out old hard-to-find model railway accessories...and the stock room two floors above the abandoned and shuttered old toy shop in the village. What treasures may be found in boxes on high dusty shelves there – among the fragile discoloured or faded bills and invoices.

Andy on Olivia

Andy, the ex-partner, says: I found it difficult to understand her - her decisions and reasons for doing what she does.

When we were "together" - when her life centred around caring for Andrew - I suppose I was too busy with my job, wanting to be the good provider, to show that she didn't have to work to bring in money. And she so loved being with him, getting to know the little character we had created between us. But it was not enough for her, and even if she didn't know it, she had a need - a hunger - for Max's approval. And that would only be achieved by working to forward his great projects.

At yet at the same time she was imagining a project of her own: the creation somehow of a world that could include Andrew's little dream of what began as mere toy trains and stations.

The whole time we were a family, these things were fermenting and maturing in some hidden place, growing steadily stronger like a buddleia under the tarmac of a country station car park, until it became unstoppable. All that energy attracted people to it, to her, like a magnet, and people found themselves ready and eager to contribute to the vision. They trusted her enthusiasm even if they didn't share the whole picture that was at the back of her mind.

The truth is, perhaps, that Olivia is somehow a reincarnation of Zoë.

Poor old General Otto

His thoughts went back.

I am, said Otto, excessively proud of my whiskers (not that I would dream of admitting as much to anyone at all). As a young man they were a fine dark colour, almost black, but by the time you knew me they had inexplicably turned to this rather striking snow white that everyone recognizes. Or is it the Emperor Franz Josef they think they are recognizing?

Otto consciously or not, secretly or not, modelled himself on his hero Napoleon. Except for the whiskers.

Otto, at the age of eighty, virtually retires to live in a hotel on the Seaglass esplanade. He finds the sound of the waves breaking on the shingle outside his high-ceilinged room helps him to relax and dulls the pain in his leg so he can get a little sleep. His breathing synchronising to the cycle of sea sounds. Sigh breathing in, soft roar breathing out...

Rex to Max

ROME

Father,

We don't seem to get much chance to talk these days, hence this, to maybe catch up. First, some confessions (not sure there's anyone else I could bring myself to confess to. The Catholic priests here seem completely alien, and would probably find it difficult to believe who I am. Whether they believed me or nor, it would put us on a very strange footing straight away). I'm not, you'll be relieved to learn, going to complain about the job you have given me. I enjoy the power, and the many perks, and I love working with Olivia – good choice for that job, if I may say so. We spent a couple of days in Rome together last week. She is a delightful person, and anyone would like to spend time with her. She is funny, tough and very perceptive. Most of the time she seems to know exactly what is good for you – even when you don't. She knows what she likes, and if she likes you, your world immediately expands considerably in every way. And she's a whiz with the Italian language. Am I allowed to contemplate the idea of marriage? And you remember saying we must not let anyone know who we really are? Are you quite sure that's the best way?

Mother Sparrow and the cat

"Come on, kids, we've overslept again. We'll be late. We're going to the jasmine garden for peanuts for breakfast. There's no bread (at least there was none yesterday), but there's nearly always nuts - even if the rats have been at them. Come on. Look, there's young blue tit going already. Cat'll get him. Nice to see Robin back. Shame he's so shy. I suppose we all overwhelm him a bit."

Little sparrow: "I like the jasmine garden. I liked the mouldy bread. With the seeds. Where's that cat? Mom, Mom, why do they call us the sparrow mafia, Mom?"

Mother: "Because there's so many of us and we don't stay still and you lot are always squabbling. And we look out for our own, son. Hey up, there's the great tit, looking smart. New moult, I see. I knew it was getting colder in the mornings."

Dad: "They call us the sparrow mafia because we are a family and we stick together. And because it sounds good and because we own the peanut feeder."

White cat: I hate those rats – smelly pleonectic creatures. I kill them if I can get in quick, when I catch them by surprise. The man here seems all right. Sometimes he fusses me while he tells me I am not to eat the robins or the wrens. Sometimes he will bang the window at me when he thinks I'm stalking a bird. He puts out peanuts which brings me the birds but also the rat family, who are very busy in the garden at night.

Ben's trouser button

Ben was entranced by the button on the front of what he thought of as his serviceable blue trousers. They were cheap - indeed they had probably been reduced in some kind of sale at the supermarket - so nothing special. Comfortable, and they seemed hard-wearing, and of an unremarkable darkish blue. What caught his eye about the button was the off-centre swirly pattern of lightish greyish colour in the plastic of the quite ordinary toffee-brown button. Once he noticed it and how it pleased him, he checked the second button, on the back pocket - but the pattern in that was not at all interesting. He had always known (well, ever since the time in his early teens when he had his first pair of glasses) that he was a little shortsighted. He delighted in small things. And quite often failed to see the bigger picture...and yet...and yet there were times when all he could see was the big picture. His parents would tell him off for making what they called "wild" sweeping generalisations - especially when he had not found convincing evidence to support his ideas. "Going off at half-cock" was what his Dad called it, urging the boy to find out more facts before drawing a conclusion or at least expressing an opinion.

Burning decks

A frosty night. Bright starlight. Harold was on the hillside behind the house, burning his collection of tarot decks. All of them - except for the deck he planned to post to his friend Millicent.

A month later, people in the village were still troubled to be finding charred fragments of cards in their gardens, with half a picture of a lion, a naked dancer or a leering portrait of a chained figure with horns and hooves.

Ben (as George junior) or indeed Harold

I'm George Benjamin Harper. For most of this story I have been either a small boy or a young teenager, though that word had hardly been invented when I became one. My Dad was George Bernard Harper. (I was well past middle age when I began to wonder about the intellect and hang-ups of a man who gave his son the same name as himself – which I suppose says as much about me as about him.) As a child I was addicted, it seems, to daydreaming. I still am, though "addicted" might be putting it a bit strongly these days – I guess I channel it more than I used to.

At school, I was nicknamed Dozy, which says it all, really. I was also, at the time this book "opens" (if it does) addicted to wearing a kind of non-Boy Scout Boy Scout outfit (without the hat, badges or woggle) of a khaki drill shirt and shorts, with grey school socks and some footwear called, I believe, sandal-shoes, that I thought were the very thing. Come to think of it, it's possible that my mother had bought me the shirts and shorts when she hoped I might indeed become a Boy Scout. I was told that I came late to the family, an "afterthought" as I think my parents put it delicately to me, after two daughters, and I think my mother (and to a large extent my father, though in a different way) had no idea how to deal with a son. I suspect that when I began to show signs of having reached what they would have thought of as the 'difficult' age, my poor dear mother would have consulted her beloved Uncle Felix, who had not only had wide experience of the world but had once been a Scoutmaster, for advice and support. On the strength of which I was dispatched to see if I would join the local Scout troop.

My sisters had both been Girl Guides – rising (presumably through the ranks – and I vaguely remember talk of Primrose Patrol and someone becoming a Patrol Leader) to be, in later years, the local Guide Captain and Lieutenant, respectively. I remember myself attending a couple of Scout meetings as a probationer (tenderfoot is, I remember, the term), sitting cross-legged on the floor of the scout hut in front of the local totem – a crudely carved wooden wolf painted black – and deciding (or it being decided for me) that I was, regrettably, not Boy Scout material. But that didn't stop me from wearing my khaki shirt, shorts and sandal-shoes as my holiday "uniform" and feeling I cut quite an acceptable figure in them.

But I digress…

Ben had wanted a real electric train set from the moment he first knew such things existed. It had been a frustration to him and his parents that he had somehow believed, as children do, that it was only ignorance and bad management that prevented it from happening. Despite his "knowing" his father only earned seven pounds a week, he couldn't at the age of say, eight, grasp the fiscal realities.

Eric's self-justifications

Eric has always gone through life justifying his actions, because his wife (and probably his mother) always seemed and seems to be criticising or attacking or challenging what he did and does. Seeing a moral dimension in every single damn thing.

Harold: The colours of war

The photographs of the period give us a false picture of the battlefields of the American Civil War. The actual scene must have been full of the colour green – not the sepia we see in the photos that makes us imagine it to be nothing but muddy – and the sound of birds on the breeze and in the bushes and trees until shocked into silence by the sudden cannon and the exploding shells. For earlier wars the visual evidence may be even less reliable.

Thinking still of the birds' song and the bangs and the silence, he lay back down in the dark and listened to his hissing tinnitus like the sound of the sea on shingle.

This is starting to feel a bit like Time Team, as if I've been excavating puzzling bits of an archaeological site that don't have any obvious connection with each other, but I'm finally beginning to see a bigger picture emerging. Or like the old one about the sculptor chipping away all the bits that are not horse to release the horse that already exists in the block of stone. And of course the story takes place in an AU where I'm the Chief of Police, where history and the rules of time and space are different, but I'm not going to say so. I'm making up back story as I go along, but quite soon I'm going to have to write it down. Or at least draw myself a diagram. Hmm, let's see...Harold Thing was the worst Police Chief in the history of Pleasant Valley but, since the Mayor was his brother in law, that was not going to change any time soon. See? Already now Zozo has become Harold's sister and married to Cecil Purehart, the Mayor of 'this burg'. Which implies a whole chunk of story that I know quite well.

I, Olivia

Some people, I know, see me as pretty arrogant, but I remember my old design tutor remarking that an artist needs to be arrogant (and God knows, she was arrogant, all right). I am, after all, continuing to be a creative person: I am still working on the several worlds I have made: the seaside triangle with its Victorian quarter, that slice of Italy behind the colosseum, the snowy forest world up under the mountain backdrop...

Ben: Courtly love

Getting bitten on the nose by that dog while trailing home after school via an unbelievably roundabout route with his mate David Sutton in order to continually swoon over the impressively older Juliet Alabaster like a lovesick medieval squire... getting bitten was clearly a shamanistic ordeal to wake him from the sleep and dozy dream of unreal courtly love he had fallen into.

A man would decide to love a lady. He would get her attention, wear her colours and fight for her in tournaments.

Week after week after afternoon school on the days when the big girls had netball or hockey practice, these two schoolboys would hang about waiting disconsolately, hoping that their chosen paramour, the girl Juliet with the hair and the eyebrows and the air of barely acknowledging their wormlike existence, would appear and would be walking home with her friend Claudette, and that they would be scornfully permitted to trail along shadowing them on the opposite side of the street, all the way along Runnings Lane right to what was really the edge of Sparkhill, or Sparkbrook or Camp Hill or wherever, where, after a long parting conversation between the girls, Claudette and Juliet would mount their bikes and ride off home in their two separate directions, leaving the two gormless boys to their own unimaginative devices.

Eric on the dolls

I wanted to be a music man. I'm a history man, I'm a teacher, I'm - lo and behold! - once more a lover after all these years. And I begin to see how little I know – certainly how little I still know, that I used to know. And I used to think I knew everything there was to know that was worth knowing.

Before I put my glasses on, in the half-light of morning, the expressions on the faces of the three dolls seated across the room seem to change all the time, as if they are all thinking, or even talking animatedly among themselves.

Planning a party

He wondered, when he was mentally fantasizing about how he would one day set up his own model railway or Scalextric layout, whether it might be possible to have one room of a model house in the Layout lit in such a way as to simulate candlelight as though it was ready for a party of some sort. Who knows – if he did that, built the house and lit it and laid out the miniature table and sideboards with miniature plaster-of-Paris quiches and bowls of punch and bunches of tiny pinhead-size grapes, who is to say that tiny double O size people in tiny party clothes driving shiny little double O scale cars might not come like Kevin Costner's dream team and ring to be admitted, bearing presents for the host?

This other gathering could be a party and a half if I could pull it off – some of the toy soldiers could attend, and he could invite Otto / the General and maybe even poor old brass Napoleon. If he could get through the door, that is. The two of them could have a discussion about ankle injuries, prosthetic feet and surgical boots. And maybe the red-eyed rabbit from his office desk drawer to add a whole other dimension and bring in mental health to the conversations.

Ben grew up (what with Dad having been in the RAF, and where there were aircraft recognition magazines in the house, brought, I think, by Dad's Air Force friend 'Uncle' Bill) to be a bit of a plane spotter, taking an interest and a pride in being able to identify most of the aircraft that flew over the house. To that end he had a telescope. Nothing ambitious, but efficient enough to allow him to make out the individual tiles on the roofs of houses two streets away. A possibly interesting relationship exists between this and his fascination with model buildings. And of course, it's almost certainly a psychological truism (is that the word I want?) that people – men primarily – who are, or feel they are, powerless in their everyday life will seek or create a "model world" – Scalextric, model railways, wargaming, computer games now – in which they are able to exercise more or less total control.

There's a programme on the Discovery Shed channel called Model Town, that Ben actually loves to watch. It's a programme that gives technical demonstrations of how to create model landscapes to go alongside the trains in a model railway. Presented in quite a jokey, blokeish (but still you can't avoid being a bit basically anorak when you enthuse however ironically about baseboards and dyed flock* – ask Olivia) style, it will, for instance show us how to install a model ruined castle on or in a model hillside, and goes on to demonstrate ways to not only fit a scale model ghost in a window of the castle but also how to make a spooky pale blue light shine on or through the ghost when someone should approach the castle.

I suspect that it's a programme that Max might also enjoy. Not sure how Martin might react to it. He might finally lose his mind. Olivia would watch it with half an eye while attending to something else on a Sunday morning – at her house? At Rex's mother's (helping get the lunch together? Even Christmas lunch? What would they have? This is the sort of question that leads novelists, I suppose, to do serious research that results in all those acknowledgements)

* The fact is – Olivia's enthusiasm drags in other people. It's like an energy magnet and other people are – oh, I don't know – iron filings or something, sucked in willy-nilly. Like that absurd boss of

hers just giving her that whole enormous old Bulfinch Retreat house to rattle around in.

The dimming of the gods

Eric is reading about Bruckner – "half simpleton, half god" and a devout Catholic – not unlike the way Margot turned out to be?

And Mahler. Brought up in a little village hundreds of miles out in the wilds that just happened to have barracks in it. Gave up his Jewishness in order to take over the Opera in Vienna.

The ballet in *Oklahoma!* adds to the music and lyrics further insights into the psychological state of the characters. *Carousel* is the carousel we are all on.

The Hapsburg Empire was ruled by Hans Joseph from the age of 18 when he was placed on the throne as Emperor. Was it the Hapsburg dynasty who were the patrons of the painter with the Dali moustache – so to speak – who is in Las Meninas? Velazquez of course. The inbred kings with the long chins and the weak and curling lips.

XII

Feet of clay

Rex says to Liv one day, "If you ever start to feel bored or dizzy on that pedestal I have put you on, just let me know and I'll see if I can help you down from it."

ZZZRRT

I sometimes (Wow - a dragonfly! That was close) wonder whether I have been sent back here from the future - say next Tuesday sennight – or possibly from the past, to try to find out why things got so bad: when the decline began, when the rot started. Observe and report back (forward) on how things have developed since our time: have the cockroaches taken over the world yet...?

I LERVE hexagons. I loved growing up being ZZZRRT snug in my cell. Is life just a dream?

Hello - what's this spoiled brat up to, making pictures of swarms of men dressed up as insects? Ah, look, he's discovering hexagons and optimal snugness. Could be the future.

Aaaah - smooooke...zzzzzzzzzzz

OCD

The world is full of things that need tidying up. You can't tidy them all up in the real world, but on the Layout, you might be able to eventually make everything tidy and perfect – or imperfect but controlled, as Capability Brown tidied up trees and water to create his vision of perfect landscapes.

Ben looking in the hotel mirror

I see someone in the process of growing up, growing out of his childhood. It's probably too late for him to become an adult in this lifetime, since he started so late, but he can make himself useful.

An odd hotel, this – it has a Napoleonic theme to its residents' coffee lounge, as a gesture to the building's history. It was apparently a hospital for French officer prisoners-of-war. So on the walls between the glass-fronted cupboards housing someone's once-precious regiments of model soldiers, Scrabble sets, jigsaws and out-of-date touring guides, meant to beguile away rainy days, are prints of dashing French light cavalrymen on manoeuvres and several moody depictions of Bonaparte on board the Bellerophon – the ship that took him to exile, apparently named after a great hero and monster-slayer in ancient Greece - and at St Helena.

Dr Downey's animal inventory

In his mind's eye (he was not daft enough to actually walk from room to room - though he just might do that at the end - to make certain he had not overlooked something obvious) Eric checked out each horizontal surface in the bungalow, taking stock of every example of inanimate life-form.

Here's some of what he found during his stocktaking:

In the bedroom, a Welsh sheep, a lamb, a leopard, a rabbit and a little white dog; in the boxroom, an elephant and a monkey; in the sitting room, another two elephants, three donkeys, a hedgehog full of biros, two young stags, a zebra and a tiger. Oh, and a white camel teapot and a Tiffany-type coloured glass mosaic frog with a light inside.

Harold on religion and rubbish

Was he beginning to get over some of his hang-ups, since starting to keep a journal? The rubbish, for instance, was beginning not to bother him so much. Yesterday evening he had taken out the small brown plastic Kitchen Waste box with its brown paper bag almost overflowing with a week's sprout trimmings, teabags and heaven knows what other excelsior – that even last month he would have hated to have to handle in case the soggy bottom of the bag fell out and dumped mouldy bread and wet bathroom-floor-hairs and worse on the hall carpet or his shoes…but now it was just a matter-of-fact job that had to be done, albeit carefully to avoid making a mess, and so with no fuss he carefully did it. like a Quaker would, he thought…He had great admiration for what he thought of as the quietly efficient approach Quakers took to life.

Mistakenly, he supposed, he had come to associate Quakerism with a sort of humanism – almost an agnosticism, certainly "low church", in those terms, by comparison with the incense-swinging Anglicanism of the church his parents had made him attend whenever an alibi could not be found or invented. His idea came from his friend Madders, whose manner seemed to come from a family background of calm logic based on unemotional assessment of the facts of a given situation - in strong contrast to the way decisions at Ben's home were arrived at – through emotional blackmail and spurious appeals to often vague abstract, theoretical or often frankly sophistical (is that even a word?), not to say transparently spurious, arguments.

Floaters

When I look up at the pale grey sky - swarms like the Somerset Levels' starlings gathering to roost, of tiny black rings each with a black dot in the centre, flow across my field of vision in two or more layers, as of the planetary spheres.

In the course of one night

In the theatre of dreams, we can attend the equivalent of a week or even a whole season of repertory theatre productions - up to half a dozen assorted stage performances that on first sight seem completely unrelated to each other and with wildly differing and bizarre settings and entirely different casts of characters.

That is the kind of experience I wish to present in my book - a bunch of glimpses into dramas whose connections, if any, may not be easy to discern, and whose "meaning" is open to interpretation - often all but as impenetrable as the forest itself. The forest on the hills at the back of the Layout extends into a photo mural of endless Canadian conifers, with an occasional stretch of water, masquerading as the Great Mid-European Forest.

Olivia and Rex

Not quite siblings, not quite lovers.

By the pond

I remember the day when the dragonfly came, said Ben. A hot still day it must have been. I can feel the hot moist air by the grey pond in Uncle Felix's garden. I was doing nothing in particular, as far as I remember. Maybe thinking about helicopters. Wasn't there a film? There was! Gregory Peck. Nineteen fifty something. The Korean War. His jet was shot down – a Hawker Hunter, like the one I laboriously made a model of at school in the Model Aero Club our beloved form master Mr Pritchett started – only navy blue. Or was it an American plane with 'Navy' on the wing in white? Like the one I made from a plastic kit when I was really too old to be doing such things, but I liked its lines. A Grumman - not a Hellcat and not, I think, a Tomcat. That had straight wings – this was swept-wing. One of their carrier fighters, anyway. Grumman Cougar. Probably.

Anyway. Daydreaming by the pond and there was the dragonfly. A gigantic one. I must have held out my hand for it. Uncle Felix's tranquillity had got to me and I was not afraid. Kind of knew it might land on my hand if I kept still. In those days I could keep still like a stone or a statue if I wanted to. My sister had given me an illustrated book about Mondrian and I had begun to sometimes understand things.

And yes, he settled on my hand. I remember feeling the weight of him, a really big one, beautiful. Pale blue-green and brown pattern all along his stick-like long body – the colours reminded me forcibly of a dreadful knitted wool one-piece bathing suit my mother had made me when I was probably four, using wool no doubt unknitted from two other previous garments. It soaked up seawater and drooped in a horrible, stretched and uncomfortable way, and I hated it. I remember the dragonfly's head with its enormous eyes, swivelling. The eyes like the cabin of a Bell helicopter, the big muscular clump of his shoulders like the mechanism that powers a helicopter's blades. I sat very still and he stayed while I admired him there on the palm of my hand.

Suddenly, though, a revulsion – a feeling he was alien. Not quite a fear of being bitten (though I could see his jaws – that would catch and eat his prey) but I could not stand him being there for a second more, and I flung my hand away from me. I hope he didn't dash his brains out on the concrete rim of the pond – I don't remember seeing where he went – but he was gone. And instantly I was filled with remorse. Guilty, and as ashamed as later, when I was on a camping holiday in the Scilly Isles with my school friends Owen and Brush, I shot a sparrow from a branch with Brush's air rifle.

Understanding Eric

Eric had trained himself, whenever he was wide awake in the small hours and unable to sleep, to pay attention to his breathing and visualise waves breaking on a shingle beach such as Sidmouth, synchronising the image with the pattern of his breath – so that as he breathed in he saw the water pulled away by gravity and felt the suck as it receded past his naked toes through the slope of fine pebbles and then, as his in-breath peaked and paused, he saw the wave beginning to crest and tip over at the top before crashing down, with more or less force depending on the strength of his breath, to coincide with his slightly noisy out-breath. This pattern usually only had the chance to repeat a few times before he was fast asleep and oblivious or dreaming.

Baptised Ludwig

Ludwig was such a dabbler (what some people would call a dilettante). For some of the people in this book the year was 1959: for Ludwig it was about 1825. At the very latest. Probably much, much earlier.

I love my soldiers. I will love my daughter. My mother told me many things, some of which were true and some of which may still be true, and some of which I know were fibs – though she may have believed some of them. It's all rather confusing. I tried to hold it together with Schnee.

Olivia examining Martin

Liv lay Martin on his back on her work table, flipped down her magnifying spectacles with the built-in LED light [which may not yet have been invented] and peered into his tiny face.

Little man, little man, she asked out loud, what is going on inside your tiny head?

Camellia sinensis

"We should have brought one of the laptops with us. Then we could have looked up these things."

"I told you to bring a computer."

"No, you didn't. You said should we and I said no – I thought it was a daft idea, but I was wrong. I thought it would do us good to have a few days away without our smartphones and computers."

For some reason I seemed to have been thinking about China tea – Ah, I know why: remembering my Great Uncle Felix, who had lived for some time in China and had introduced and taught me to appreciate the dry and slightly acerbic taste of what he called black tea – mixing his own blend of 'ordinary' tea with the black woody leaves be bought in bulk and that smelled of what I now knew to be probably bergamot.

I thought I remembered reading the name *Sinensis* on the picture on the wall of the hotel room – a print of a white rose, framed in a narrow gilt frame with a broad pink mount that, along with the small writing-desk where you wrote your three or four postcards to friends, gave the impression of slightly gracious living. Not that we live ungraciously when we are at home. But I checked and found I had been mistaken – it actually read *Bengale Thé Hymenée* (what on earth does that mean – Bengal tea with a hymen? How weird – are these accommodations meant to be a bridal suite?).

I knew the tea plant was a kind of Camellia. Or is it Camelia? Sounds better. La Dame aux…

Counselling

"In that strange subjunctive universe that is the only one in which your question could have any meaning, yes - it is your fault that the women with whom you fall in love are married to other people. You should have married one of them yourself first."

He looks out of the window. "Looks like the Sparrers have come in a charabanc – a sparrer charra."

She is either not amused or fails to understand. Or is simply no longer listening as she watches the scenery flow past the train window.

Travel light

I have in my head now this list of things I have to do that I can do. This is unusual. What happened to all the things I didn't know how to do? The only one I can remember was solved by simply waiting until the other person involved in doing it got back home, read my email and responded/ said they would do it. Moral: Wait and let other people do their part. Travel a bit more lightly.

A bedtime story

There once was a man called On Tuan Dersant Egg Soup Airy, she told her little boy at bedtime, who used to fly a blue French aeroplane over hundreds of miles of Algerian desert. As he flew his aeroplane high up in the cold air with nothing to see but sand and sky, hour after hour all alone, he would make up stories about a planet and a little man who lived on the planet.

The weather on the planet would slowly change, sometimes very cold for a few thousand years, then really warm for thousands of years.

The people who lived on the planet at one time decided that the way to organise things was to have two different kings – one who wanted everyone to have a comfortable, safe kind of life, and one who wanted his friends to become very very rich and powerful indeed and didn't care about the lives of people who were not rich and powerful. The idea was for one king to be in charge for a few years and try to arrange things so that his plans worked out, and then for the other king to have a go at being in charge for a few years. As you can imagine, it was not a happy planet.

The problem was that each king's friends used to do their best to prevent the other king from getting his own way. Gradually, matters became worse and worse as the rich and powerful king's friends spoiled more and more of the once beautiful planet by digging mines, looking for precious metal to make coins, and cutting down forests to make fields for cattle for meat.

XIII

Chinaman's sleeves

When Ben wanted to be sure of a couple of hours of sleep to dream a solution to something troubling him, or at least to drift into a meditative and relaxed state, he would have three or four ginger nut biscuits with a drink of water or something stronger and go back to bed in his dressing gown, tucking his hands inside the opposite sleeves like the chinaman in the Rupert Bear books. It vaguely felt like a way of balancing left and right brain functions, ying and yang, or maybe recycling the chi energy round his body. It was also comforting and kept his hands warm.

A one-sided conversation

"I sometimes feel as though you have created me. I don't think you even know my name - I'm not even at this moment certain that I know my own name or remember it. I know your name - you're The Mistress, my maker. To you I'm probably just the porter who hoes his vegetable patch. You've spent time creating me, painting my tiny face and the white dots on my red kerchief, and from time to time, when the whim takes you, you will come in here, switch on the light and "play" with me as if poking me with a stick through the bars of my invisible cage. You'll move me about, maybe change the colour of my boots, put me out in the road or see if you can fit me into the kitchen through the little door and then, when you get bored or some other way of passing your time occurs to you, off you'll go and leave me standing or lying where you last put me, to wait until the next time you decide to make something really happen in my little universe."

Olivia up in the air

Whoops! Oh, here we go again. So I'm in a plane. Is it my plane? (I do seem to be flying it, and I also seem, oddly but very comfortingly, to know what I'm doing.) I must say, scary though it can be for moments at a time when I find myself suddenly in situations like this one, I love my job. So exciting and fulfilling.

Otto at Bad Gödesborg Station

The railway station at Bad Gödesborg, the town nestling under the threatening but also protective shadow of the crowned double-headed eagle, looking out fierce and imperious in both directions over the alps – the great Bernstein peak that was bringing new tourists and climbers to patronize the chalet-shops selling lederhosen and alpenstocks and fine hats with brave plumes. The station had been the scene of Otto's greatest triumphs over the years - going off to militärisch gymnasium with his splendid black whiskers, and returning resplendent in a golden pickelhaube to bring his wonderful torpedo design, but then back again after receiving his dreadful wound, his whiskers gone absolutely white and his torpedo a failure. Still proud, still loved by the local women and admired by the men - that fiasco somehow engineered, they were sure, by a conspiring cabal of envious fellow officers.

Rex

The brittle but somehow damped shell-like sound of the teapot lid going back on, after he had lifted it to stir the tea, transported him directly back to the veranda of the Hotel Schloss Bernstein and reminded him of the week they had spent there apeing the behaviour of nobility or at least gentry that might not anymore actually exist. Bernstein had originally been in Hungary but at the period when they were there it was considered to be in Austria, as "since the war...they moved the border a few miles." The place had been like a time warp, but they had had a truly great time as incognito tourists...

He remembers the five-sided room of the camera obscura at the top of the ancient castle, high up among the turrets, where images were cast on the walls showing the five different views – a glimpse of the loggers' camp among the pine trees and the dense forest, stretching away to the snowy peaks of the Carpathians beyond; when the sun broke through, another window showed distant Kaliningrad gleaming, an amber jewel dropped into the distant blank expanse of steppe; turning from that, one saw a sharply detailed image of the grand front of the railway terminus (surely inspired by St Mark's in Venice), while in another direction one had a sniper's view of tiny characters going about their secret lives down in the wide main street of the town below.

Postscript

Obviously, clearly, a tying up of loose ends, almost a fresh start. We have one group, Mundy, Mundy and Vogel, the architectural practice with offices in Fallerton. Max and Rex, father and son, are architect and quantity surveyor respectively, I believe. Olivia is an architectural model maker.

Also long-established just outside the town are the family of powerful women – Schnee (The Princess Schneegwyn Esterhazy-Swanning von Lozin und Bernstein), Susan, Jean, and Daphne. Their bloodline can be traced back to the female founders of the amber mining concern (based on the Lozin mine outside Bernstein, Austria) from which the town traditionally derives its prosperity. Martin has married into this matriarchy.

Ben's family forms a third group – him, his parents and his mother's uncle Felix. Owen and Nigel are bit players here.

We also have a group of three girls, Hen, Zo, and Margot. Zo is almost certainly the daughter of Ludwig, known as Louis, who was married to one of the Faller women.

Otto and Eric represent separate threads – Eric was one of Ben's teachers and has been befriended by Hen. Harold is a writer. Otto is a retired General, and Ludwig's great-uncle.

Later in the day, the main attractive characters will be seen as a sort of tableau vivant, derived from Hollywood musical poster imagery, bouncing arm in arm or hand in hand down the brightly lit hillside like something from The Wizard of Oz or The Sound of Music – Olivia, Rex, Henrietta and Eric or, in an alternative scenario, Ben, Martin, Jean and Olivia plus perhaps the three "dolls" – in the style of Dorothy, the Cowardly Lion and the Tin Man.

We still don't know where Hen and Margot came from. I think they are Faller cousins, but they may both have been adopted – by Susan or Schnee. Does it matter? (always with the kvestions!) I can't quite bring myself to approach Max (who must know – surely) to find out.

Susan

I suppose I'm still Susan...yes, that sad creature. But I'm not at all. Sad, that is. Hope I never lose this joy in life, in tiny things, wonderful people, colour and strange things, and the sense of wonder at this astonishing universe of ours. I do love being alive. So much to fascinate, to care about, and I'm still on my bike at least once a week going to see my gorgeous, serious, brave daughter and my amazing granddaughter, who is going to carry on the family traditions: I can feel it in my bones and see it in her eyes, so bright, like a bird's. So eager to learn and to understand. Oh, the stories I shall be able to tell her, about princesses shut up in towers and rescued by handsome princes, and about all the strong clever women she is descended from. Men are a disappointment, by and large, for all sorts of reasons they don't seem able to help, but the women in this family won't let you down.

A dream of winning a million pounds

George the younger [Ben, or maybe Harold] dreamed that he had won a million pounds in the lottery. In the dream, he was obviously happy and made preparations for spending some of the money on a house and wondering what else to do with the rest of it. They could go on a foreign holiday again, maybe go, on a plane this time, to Italy again – only Pru or Mrs Thing wouldn't really be able to do any walking, couldn't actually cope with getting about the airport and on and off the aircraft, really. They could buy a new car – though the one they had was less than a year old. Mainly, he supposed, he could get on with doing the various things he had been putting off, like learning to play the piano with proper lessons, maybe finally accept that there was no point in keeping the old paintings of his that were in the shed, since none of his work was likely to sell – even if he had the energy or motivation to show or advertise it. And he could get rid of the old bike he was never – let's face it – going to ride again. And he might as well clear out the boxes of poetry books he didn't want for anything.

When he woke up and realized it had been just a dream, he lay quietly for a few minutes letting it sink in, then got up and moved the big carton full of poetry books down the stairs. Later in the day, he put them in the car and took them to the Oxfam shop. That night he found himself thinking about the model railway layout he had once planned to build in the spare room. He had actually been more interested in the model cars and the roadway that he had intended to create around and alongside the railway part of it. The firm that had made the roadway, Minic Raceways, had long ago now gone out of business, but he had for quite a long time collected bits of the track and other accessories by ordering them by post from various people who still possessed surprising amounts of the things and would advertise them in a kind of newsletter he had tracked down. He couldn't now remember the details, but with the internet, he ought to be able to look it up and see what might still be available. He imagined there must still be a few people about - think of how many spoiled and indulged sons of well-off parents there would have been in, say, the whole of Yorkshire - who would have badgered their doting Mums and Dads to give them those lovely cars and roads to go with their model railways. In the morning he would start searching. He turned over and went back to sleep.

Mistress > shrink

Every Wednesday he went straight from visiting his mistress to visiting his psychotherapist. For about five minutes he thought himself a very fine fellow. It might have been more helpful to organize his day the opposite way round.

Optimum packing...

the "work" he did with his coins as a boy, seeing how many would go into a given circular area, had a serious civil engineering application in calculating how to bundle steel cables into the supports for the carriageway of a suspension bridge, and much later in life Ben/Ludwig made a small fortune applying his informal research.

A schwa person

Either Eric or Martin/Ben (or both or all three - and perhaps I will admit somewhere that most of my characters are interchangeable or aspects of an ur-character based, natürlich, on myself) feel themselves to be a sort of schwa person. They are occupied in this life with fathoming out a unified theory of existence (is life really a dream, etc.) and only incidentally take jobs in teaching or on the railway and happen to collect a doctorate or fatherhood in passing. But posterity will perhaps know them as major thinkers or figures in the history of philosophy who did not have any profession other than that of thinker.

Something not quite right here

Every morning she stood at her window at the top of the house and watched as the narrowboat chugged slowly round the bend in the canal below, and every evening she waited for its return, imagining the life and character of the man at the tiller. She also looked out every morning for the sleek yellow Citroën "La Poste" van to sweep over the bridge, hoping for a letter.

He goes through life like Epaminondas in the children's book

Learning every life lesson too late, telling beautiful women (the only kind there are, when you come down to it) he wants to spend the night with them - which would have been bad enough, but in his case, the appalling truth is that he means it. Every time he falls in love he forgets the previous love.

He miscalculates all the time – when adding up or multiplying figures (especially cash) but also more generally – not only dangerously, when driving, but also in relationships, and he never seemed to learn from his mistakes.

He often feels himself to be invisible to other people – except to his mother, who doesn't count. Yet he is also generally bigger than Godzilla.

Like Salinger's Seymour Glass, he feels he might be "a kind of paranoiac in reverse. I suspect people of plotting to make me happy."

About a toy

Which of these people – Martin the dutiful young husband agonising about ambition; pompous Eric besotted with his Henrietta; Ben the man of putty; dynamic Owen; pure-hearted Rex – would be most worth asking whether they remembered the strange simple circus toy, roughly the size of the round box that cheese triangles came in, only deeper, with a transparent lid of thick cellophane and the tiny figures, like determined little paper actors with no script or director, aimlessly twirling about in static electricity whenever we rubbed our fingers over the top? Was it in fact, meant to be a circus? There was an audience represented all around the inside. It was not, I think, meant to be merely a football match. Or perhaps they were skaters. We had it for years knocking about in our bedrooms and toy-cupboards – one of those casual toys one would pick up and idly play with, for a few minutes maybe every few weeks, and then put down or put away and forget about again. But it seemed magical and haphazard in its operation, enchantingly unpredictable and light-hearted and purposeless. A proper toy. Thinking about it again as I re-read this, it seems more and more likely they were meant to be skaters. Surely the bottom inside the thing was silver, like a small cake-board, and represented the ice rink?

Later: I just found a couple for sale on eBay – turns out it's called a Magico 'Rub-it' toy. The ones on offer are either a circus with clowns, or an underwater scene with a diver and a crocodile –

though I'm pretty sure the one I remember featured skaters in an ice-rink. Same principle as the amber rod we were sometimes shown in school science lessons, rubbed with a silk cloth and picking up scraps of paper to demonstrate the mysterious force of static.

From Downey's secret journal

I'm well aware that a lot of people don't very much like me. I used to tell myself it was because they envied my intelligence. The superior mind always makes its possessor somewhat of an outsider. And, yes, I know I lack the social graces and the knack some of my more relaxed colleagues have, of creating an easy familiarity with people when I first meet them – particularly women, I suppose – unless we share an interest or a level of subject expertise, in music history, obviously, or any of the other fields with which I'm familiar. I don't know if you've ever had the experience of meeting a person who seems to have something really extraordinary about them. It may, I suppose, be a particular sensitivity about me, but there have been two or three occasions in my life when I have - not even 'met' them in the sense of speaking to them or shaking their hand, but encountered I suppose is the word to use – encountered someone who struck me as different from normal people. If I believed in aliens, I would say if there were aliens living among us, I may have seen four of them. Or angels, perhaps. The first time it happened, I suppose I realize now, could have been largely an effect of the light. I was in Grey Street, in Newcastle upon Tyne. I remember, when turning a corner, I almost bumped into a man with the most extraordinarily luminous green eyes who was just standing there as if waiting for someone. His face was mostly shaded by the hat he was wearing, but his eyes reminded me of nothing so much as a pair of green traffic lights. We didn't speak, and I never saw him again.

I have forgotten where or when it was I saw the second person, but I do remember that we actually met and exchanged some words. He seemed, I remember, full of animation and energy and was trying (as happens at parties sometimes) to get me to share his very positive and excited views about the possibilities life offers us if we will only go all out in pursuit of our personal aims and desires. He had very dark and shining eyes, and dark curly hair. May well have been foreign - Arabic or South American perhaps, or from the Caribbean, and with eyes so dark they seemed to be all pupil and to have no distinct irises. I remember suspecting at the time that he might be on some kind of drugs. Again, I have not met him since.

More recently I have met a couple, Gaby and Mike, who have bowled me over with what I can only describe as their appetite for life. When we were introduced at Henrietta's Halloween party, it was as if they somehow knew all about me and were expecting to meet me there, so warm were their greetings.

Ages

Ben thought that one ought to be able to tell exactly what age a person is by looking carefully at them – someone such as the young mother feeding her baby girl in the Bay café-bar – by kind of analysing just how anxious or serious and guarded she was being in, for instance, not quite catching anyone's eye as they squeezed past her table on the way to the bar to pay for their cups of coffee or crab sandwiches. Her hair had been very smoothly and neatly drawn down and back from her face and she was really concentrating on the rituals of wiping milk dribbles from the baby's chin with a carefully folded cloth and moving on to spoon more solid food from a plastic container. Not all that long out of school, probably. An earnest young woman accepting her responsibility.

XIV

Harold is not Max

Max is the creator: Harold is the writer - not the same thing.

"The image is a projection of the self, made visible" (Liesl Silverstone, from *Counselling*)

Leaving it for Julia

One of the girls explains: there's an expression "leave it for Julia" that means you don't expect anything to happen. Julia's interpretation of course, is that they leave it up to Julia to decide if a thing is important enough to do something about.

I might change Henrietta's name to Julia. She is the eldest of the cousins/sisters.

Max: Do I believe in myself? I really do. Am I God?

Not sure whether this is a lingering doubt or a lingering certainty.

When I look out to the pattern of pinkish light beneath the violet clouds above the distant skyline, it all feels familiar, as if it belongs to me in some way, as if I made it.

Do I create the weather? Not day by day, no – but I might well have set in motion the system that causes the weather to behave as it does. With the help of Olivia.

And even if I didn't exactly create Olivia, I certainly made her what she has become. It's Olivia I wanted to talk about.

Eggshell-eating Otto

It was rumoured that, if given a boiled egg, he would eat it entire - shell and all. Whether this, if true, was from impatience or bravado (or was a trick he had learned in order to impress people with his iron constitution or his originality) is hard to establish.

Easier to believe in relation to those dainty blue-shelled eggs you occasionally see - or indeed of quails' eggs, which might have been served to a person of his class in those days - than of normal modern everyday hens' eggs.

Downey, as a descendant of the General, may tell this story to seem interesting to his lady love. Likewise that Ludwig or Otto once made himself ill by accidentally brushing his teeth with handcream, which bestowed on him ever after the gift of the gab and thereby contributed greatly to his success in life.

Rex, singing in the shower

Jesus is just all right with me.
Jesus is just all right, oh yeah.
Jesus is just all right with me.
Jesus is just all right…

Rex is well aware that some of his friends [I almost wrote 'disciples'] describe him as "a bit of a hippie" and are mildly amused by his occasional statement of faith, what they see as his naïve or even simple-minded trusting that there is a benign intelligence behind the universe, and that "all things are unfolding as they should." And yet, in what he thinks of as his darker moments, he does find himself seriously wondering whether life is in fact a dream, an illusion – whether we each construct from moment to moment what appears to be reality.

It's simple, Rex told the crazy Cardinal: in your world you have lots of pictures on the walls, and wooden images of Christ crucified, of the Madonna and child: in my world we have pictures of Bismarck, say, or brass statuettes of Napoleon.

Schnee: Hotels

I don't know what hotels are coming to. I used to so love being looked after by my favourite waiter and the maître d'hôtel. I suppose he would be called. All among the pictures of dashing young French cavalrymen and cuirassiers and whatnot and the aspidistras. Morning coffee, a light luncheon, afternoon tea with little cakes on the terrace listening to the waves. Maybe a little orchestra inside out of the wind. And we would wear hats. Such hats. The fun we had. A hat ('hets' we would call them) with little scraps of veil we would lift, just so, to pop in a dainty cake.

Martin and the talking bee

Maybe because over the years, when he'd come across a bumble bee on the ground, apparently either dying or starving or unable to take off and fly about its business, Martin had always tried to help the creature onto a wall or a branch from which it could once more take to the air, and because he had never really been afraid that a bee would want to sting him – unless it got trapped inside his shoe – one day a friendly talking bee had come to him (as he was sitting dozing under an apple tree by a pond) - had come and told him that, as a result of his having decided years ago in a previous incarnation as a librarian, when he had come across the title of a book (not that he'd read the book) "Pure, White and Deadly" about the evils of white sugar, he had made the decision to always have in his tea a spoonful of honey (to be totally accurate, more like half a spoonful) instead of sugar – his investment in honey had paid off, and not only did he feel that regime has made him pretty healthy, but he could now – almost as a reward or dividend – have an ability to understand the talk of bees. Maybe not.

It makes no sense, but he now knows that what a grounded bee needs is almost certainly a few drops of sugar-water (not actually honey, strangely, the RSPB says) to provide a quick energy boost, but still...

Artists and mirrors

She feels an inch tall. She has brought Andrew's double-sided shaving mirror from the bathroom and propped it at the end of the terrace of workman's houses to look at them from what would be the residents' eye level.

It's an old artists' trick that she probably learned from Felix at art school - looking at a painting or drawing in progress, or at the subject, through a mirror in order to get a fresh "eye" and spot mistakes of proportion or infelicities that you had maybe stopped noticing.

Doing this has always made her feel in some way connected, at one with the old masters - Vermeer, Durer, even Rembrandt. Now it allows her to look at the Layout from the viewpoint of its inhabitants and see how crude some of the details would look to them.

The German Submariner's Tale

One warm night in May, while Jean was in the hospital waiting for Daphne to be born, and Martin had been allowed by a sympathetic midwife to sit beside the bed and hold Jean's hand during a bit of a lull between bursts of pushing and panting, she had told him a story her grandmother Schnee had taught her, of a young German submariner in the First World War who had been serving in the South Atlantic. One quiet day at sea, he had been sunbathing on the deck when a freak wave had washed him overboard, and he had sunk like a stone, only to be rescued by a great sea dragon who had taught him to swim and had taken him down to her palace on the sea bed. She kept him imprisoned there as a cross between a servant and a pet. Eventually after a year and a day becoming tired of his constant complaints about the boring diet of fish, she let him escape to the surface, whereupon he had swum to the shore of Africa and had been rescued. He had gone on to become, for many years, a successful swimming teacher and had eventually retired to open a fishmonger's in Danzig (now Gdansk), where he would regale with his story as many of his customers as would listen.

Will the Layout ever be finished?

Will the Layout ever be finished? Olivia asks herself - not that it matters. She began making it when her son was interested in model railways, years ago, and after he had been through university and was on his way to a successful career in America, she still is in the habit of thinking about ways to make it ever more detailed, complex, "complete" and visually convincing for, she realised with a frisson of excitement, her own satisfaction.

Max's divinity

Max may not know he is God, or may not be absolutely certain of his divinity, but on his office wall is a print of William Blake's depiction of Sir Isaac Newton as the Great Architect bent double over his giant dividers.

Harold probably looked at himself in the mirror one day in his youth and wondered if he was in fact, Jesus.

The House of Mothers

- the idea Olivia picked up from the Dalai Lama, that down the course of our numberless reincarnations throughout the millennia, every soul in the world would at some time have cared for us as a mother does, and so we should give them all our compassion: these are our parents, our children.

The Bay Café-Bar

On the seafront at Lyme Regis is what describes itself as The Bay Café-Bar, an establishment with small tables both outside (bearing warnings about the fact that gulls will steal your chips or ice cream, held down against the often stiffish sea breeze by hefty pebbles from the beach) and inside out of the wind, behind large glass doors. It was in here, stroller parked alongside the table, that Rex (having driven hither on a Sunday morning whim) first caught sight of, laid eyes on, our Jean. In this instance, Jean was to all intents and purposes, by herself with her baby girl, whom she was with great and serious attention and care feeding, firstly from a bottle of, we assume, formula, and then with even more concentration, solids with a two-colour plastic spoon from a container she had brought with her, wiping the child's face between times with a large and neatly folded mustard-hued flannel. Rex, being Rex, attempted several times to catch the young woman's eye, but she was having none of it and continued quite fiercely to pay attention to what she was doing – as a young mother doubtless should. Being Rex, he also greatly approved of this maternal singlemindedness. Indeed, had it been by some weirdness of cosmology possible for the young man to select at that moment a candidate for the role of his mother, Jean would have found herself comfortably assigned first place in the running.

Rex had been peripherally aware of a young man with two little black and tan dachshunds on leads, lounging about leaning against the railings outside on the promenade as if waiting for something to happen and looking, frankly, disreputable, scruffy and, yes, a tad furtive. A number of more or less genteel and seemingly rather well-to-do couples and small groups of friends strolled past, enjoying the fresh air on this mild if blowy morning, walking a variety of dogs and generally seeming at ease with themselves, one another and the universe at large. The man with the two dogs was somehow not one of their number, his thoughts (for he did seem quite deeply in thought) apparently of a darker kind. His presence made Rex uneasy. He would have liked further insight into the man's motives and preoccupations. Rex could almost fancy that the man was a stalker, and that the object of his interest might the young mother whom Rex was also watching. In due course the young woman – carefully, unhurriedly and with a notable economy of movement, strapped her child back into the harness of the baby buggy, wiped clean and stowed away the various accoutrements she had been using, thanked the waitress for her cooperation, scanned the area around the table one last time to make sure she had not left anything behind, and manoeuvred herself and her vehicle out of the door and onto the prom, where she linked arms with the dark young man with the two dogs and headed off into the breeze.

For Olivia, it was the dandelions that did it

Driving through the lanes after Easter, Olivia notices dandelions (or they might be lesser celandines) like yellow suns and stars scattered suddenly all along the foot of the hedgerows, and finds herself wanting to hurry home and get out the yellow paint and her finest brush to dot yellow pinpoint stars all along the model roads of the Layout and transform it to Spring.

She finds herself pulling over and parking in a gateway to take it all in, winds down her window and smells the polleny scent on the breeze. Why do I have to keep on trying to perfect my Layout and make it look more real? I can't control it in every detail, I don't need to, I have the actual celandines and dandelions out here in the real world and the blossom on the trees to enjoy without picking up a single brushful of paint ever again.

A load of some kind lifts from her mind and shoulders. For the first time she feels sorry for all those blokes and boys at the model railway show who feel so powerless in front of the world they can't control, taking refuge inside the little few square feet of miniature worlds where they can be in charge.

Max drinks

Max has come down to sit quietly on the dark chocolate-coloured leather settee in his living room at three in the morning, a glass with half an inch of scotch on the coffee table in front of him and, at this moment, his head in his hands. He leans forward and breathes out a longish breath. It's all a muddle. How on earth is he supposed to manage everybody? Far from omnipotent, he usually feels entirely powerless, and his great wealth doesn't make the slightest difference. It's no help at all. He's not allowed to go back to a previous point in time and re-arrange things. He can't even ask for a list of some sort so that he can get clear in his mind who is wrestling with what problem. And all these appeals and requests and orders, really, keep coming in. It's like running an enormous charity that hardly anybody understands.

There are times when he sees clearly that the world is just one big complicated accident – a planet in danger of being completely destroyed by all these obscene walking converters – that people are no more than mobile factories, that they simply take in at one end perfectly good living material of every kind and produce at the other end – not to put too fine a point on it – shit: noxious waste and dead matter. People think they are so clever, with their languages and their books and their inventions and their plans for how to rule the world, but they are just digestive systems on legs.

They all seem to know what they want from the organisation,

what they expect him to be able to provide – just like that – but he has to weigh up everybody's needs against what would actually be good for them, best for them (and how to work that out?) and there's nobody he can talk to about the difficulties. For two pins, he would get on the phone to Olivia. It would be good to hear her sensible voice, but she might not take kindly to being woken at this time of night. He wonders if he could discuss it at all with Rex instead. Maybe tomorrow.

It wasn't this bad when he was in China. All he had to worry about in those days – apart from understanding the language – was the termites eating the files and the river pirates stealing supplies and getting tax demands out on time. And he could lock up the office and go home to bed with a quiet mind every night.

On the Yellow River

She goes out onto the balcony and starts to water the potted tulips. She fancies she feels an earth tremor, looks down and sees that the hotel is surrounded by water – orangey grey waves rippling and swelling to the horizon in every direction – that the hotel is indeed now a boat, a ship. She takes a firm grip on the rail, steadies herself and looks out again across the waves. Sees in fact that the pleasure barge – for that she now somehow knows is what it is that she is standing on – is afloat in the middle of a very wide river. Leaning on the ship's rail, she isn't doing a thing except hold the universe together.

Extraneous matter

After the young man had laboriously, painstakingly finished carving the model fishing smack to his own satisfaction, he was able to say, with the unnamed young carpenter hero of Every Boy's Book (Routledge, 1868),

> *"All made out of my own head,*
> *And wood enough left for another."*

THE END

About The Author

Leader of djembe drumming group Drum Together, TABI-endorsed Tarot card reader, retired chartered librarian & joint founder/editor of the quarterly long-running new poetry magazine Obsessed with Pipework, Herbie Johnson lives with his cat Lynxie in the Somerset village of Evercreech. His first full poetry collection 'The Feather-List Extracts' appeared in 2005. Herbie is 82.